THE

EMBRYO

John Hagen

JOHN HAGEN

Dedication

To my dearest wife, Ileana,

whose love lights up every page of my life.

JOHN HAGEN

Acknowledgment

To Neil Hansen, Paul Dennis, Ben Hansen, Steve Gallinger, Robert Rayfield, Roger Jubinville, and Sam Berman for sharing the Caribbean ocean sailing adventure with me on S/V Ileana.

Contents

About the Author

John Hagen is a retired laparoscopic surgeon living in Toronto. Working in a large community teaching hospital, he was chief of surgery and then chief of staff before retiring from surgical practice. As a passionate sailor, he spent one winter season in the Bahamas and another in the Caribbean. He spends the summers sailing on Lake Ontario from his home port of Port Credit.

Chapter 1

They were waiting for him when he arrived home after his 10-kilometer run two men in their early 40s. They were wearing jeans and white dress shirts that were tucked in. Both were about 6 feet tall. The one who talked had short blonde hair and a seven-day coarse beard. He was slightly overweight with the start of a potbelly. They were sitting on the front porch on the steps. As soon as they saw Jeremy, they stood and walked towards him.

"I'm Jeff, and this is my colleague Ray," said the pot-bellied one. "We just spoke with your wife, and she said you had gone for a run and would be back in about half an hour. We thought we would wait for you. She was sitting on the back patio with a friend. We simply told her we were from the government and wanted to speak with you. She seemed very nice and suggested we wait for you at the front."

He pulled out his identity card, as did Ray. They were from CSIS, the Canadian Security Intelligence Service. "We were hoping to have a few words with you," said Jeff. "Is this a convenient time? Would you prefer we go somewhere more private and have coffee?"

Slightly short of breath after sprinting the last 200 meters of his run, Jeremy Young said, "This is fine. We can talk now."

Jeremy took them into the office on the main floor of the house. They sat on the couch. Jeremy sat at the desk in the swivel chair and turned to face them. Jeff spoke. "Ray and I are from the Canadian Security Intelligence Service. We don't like to use telephone or emails because these are all traceable. We prefer to come directly to your home; anything we say would be confidential. Nobody will trace our conversation; the only record will be our handwritten notes. We keep these locked in a safe. We parked our car about half a mile away so we could come directly to your home and avoid inquisitive neighbors from asking you questions about us. To clarify, we are not investigating you or any of your activities."

Jeremy stared at them incredulously. He thought his past was behind him. Having just returned from the Dominican Republic on his sailboat, he was trying to adapt to life on land. The trip to Toronto took 15 days. Iona and Jeremy sailed six days from the Dominican Republic to Norfolk, Virginia. After waiting out a storm, Jeremy continued to New York City when Iona had to fly back to Toronto. He then traveled up the Hudson River to Albany. Jeremy took the mast off the boat and shipped it by truck to Oswego, New York. He motored up the lock system of the Erie Canal to Lake Ontario. Jeremy finished the 2100 nautical mile trip with a 120-mile trip across Lake Ontario. He docked **Iona Too**, their 51-foot sailboat, at the yacht club. That was one week ago.

Jeremy and Iona hoped to begin a normal life after spending the last year in the Caribbean. They had spent the past year in remote anchorages in the Leeward Islands of the Caribbean. It was effortless. They avoided curious cruisers and their gossip. The news reporters and cameras were no longer interested in them. Their story was old news. Now this.

"We are investigating Li Ming Chang," said Ray. "Here is her picture. Do you recognize her?"

Jeremy glanced at the photo. Li Ming was a pretty woman in her mid-thirties of Chinese origin. She was smiling at something and partially turned away from the camera. A wisp of black hair covered the left side of her face, blown that way by a soft gust of wind. She had the youthful, timeless appearance and beauty gifted to the Chinese. There was a mischievous sparkle in her eyes. "Yes," said Jeremy. "I recognize Li Ming."

It was three years ago. The world was struggling with the COVID-19 pandemic. Li Ming contacted Jeremy by e-mail. The request seemed innocent enough. Li Ming wanted Jeremy to give a lecture to a group of 400 Chinese surgeons in mainland China. Jeremy had traveled to China 8 times in the past ten years. He gave talks and performed surgery, showing the surgeons the latest laparoscopic and robotic techniques. It was two weeks of 5-star hotels and incredible Chinese cuisine every night. Iona and Jeremy had plenty of time to see the incredible sights of China, all paid for by the government of China.

The purpose of the trips was to share ideas, techniques, and surgical technology. This would keep the Chinese medical system on the cutting edge of medical advancements. The Chinese hospitals they visited would frequently send surgeons to Canada for six months to observe the technology. Jeremy's trainees would go to China for surgical experience. Gastric cancers were endemic in China. The Chinese had developed new techniques to cure these patients and were happy to teach the Canadian trainees. The exchange of ideas program benefitted surgeons from both countries. Then COVID hit the world. COVID-19 caused the termination of all international exchange programs. It seemed like a reasonable request to have a Zoom meeting with surgeons in China to talk about surgical techniques.

"I gave a talk using Zoom on the laparoscopic surgical management of T4 colon cancer. This was a video of a colon cancer that was stuck on the abdominal wall and into the small bowel. We did a complete resection. I showed how to put everything back together laparoscopically," said Jeremy. "The session took about 45 minutes, and I answered questions. Li Ming organized the conference and translated."

"Do you know much about her?" asked Ray.

"She was on one of the trips to China. She showed my wife and me around Shanghai," said Jeremy.

"Here is a document you signed on one of your trips," said Ray. He pulled out a photocopy of a document that was in Mandarin.

Jeremy inspected the document. "I have no idea what this says. Whenever I visited a hospital in China, there were always a lot of ceremonies. They treated me like a visiting dignitary. A signing ceremony was always a big part of the visit. The signing was to ensure there was a document to establish a relationship between my hospital and theirs. That way, I could send my trainees to them, and they could send Chinese surgeons to us."

"Let me give you a little background," said Ray. "We are mainly interested in the transfer of confidential or proprietary information to the Chinese. Some legitimate ways exist, such as bilateral agreements and open arrangements for anyone to review. Of course, some illegal methods involve stealing information. Individuals from both countries can make private agreements to share proprietary information. While sometimes not illegal, they enter a grey zone. These arrangements may not benefit Canada with the leakage of sensitive documents to China.

"Typically, the Chinese focus on individuals with proprietary information access. They then look at ways to recruit them. The medical technology sector is a highly lucrative and fast-advancing field. Our sources suggest the Chinese are looking at ways of accessing proprietary medical research from Canada."

"Well, I've never been involved with research. Everything that I have discussed in my talk was available on the Internet. There's nothing proprietary about any of it," said Jeremy.

"When she first started her company in Canada, she traded maple syrup to the Chinese. When her business switched to medical conferencing, it caused her activities to be flagged. We believe she is involved in recruiting doctors to gain confidential research information," said Ray.

"I think you may be barking up the wrong tree with me because I've got nothing to share," said Jeremy.

Ray thought about this for a minute. "This information has been very helpful for us. If you think of anything else and want to contact us, here is our phone number." They had handwritten the number on a yellow sticky. "Use a pay phone, as they cannot trace it. Do not call us on your cell phone," suggested Ray.

The two men left. Jeremy watched them walk down the street toward their car. He considered the implications of the visit from the two spies from CSIS. Although they said they were not investigating him, he was skeptical of their motives. They did not leave their business cards. It was as if they were preparing to deny the visit even occurred.

Jeremy made his way to the back patio and sat before Iona. It was a warm spring day. The sun was shining. A large, bright red umbrella protected them from the harsh rays of the afternoon sun. He recounted the conversation and asked Iona what she thought.

"There is much more to this story than they tell us," said Iona. "I think we had better get some legal advice. I see storm clouds on the horizon."

Chapter 2

Michael was looking down at Lake Ontario from his office on the 46th floor. His office was in a high-rise tower with magnificent views of the lake. A storm had rolled in from the west. The rain pelted down on the window, horizontal from the powerful storm battering the city. A flash of lightning lit up the dark skies, followed by thunder. The lake looked cold and dangerous in the storm. The wind shook the office tower slightly. He was thinking about his visit with Jeremy and Iona. They had just left after a one-hour meeting.

Michael was in his mid-60s. He had been a criminal lawyer for the past 35 years. The grey hair was thinning at the top of his head. He was 6 foot 3 inches tall and had kept fit by walking the 3 miles to work daily. He first met Jeremy Young when he was chief of surgery at the Metropolitan Hospital. The hospital paid out a generous settlement to Jeremy after Michael launched a wrongful dismissal lawsuit. This allowed Jeremy and Iona to spend a comfortable year in the Caribbean on their 51-foot sailboat. They had just returned to Toronto with their sailboat. He was confident their past troubles were behind them, but a visit from Canada's spy agency could be more trouble for them.

After looking out the floor-to-ceiling window, Michael returned to his desk and sat down. He picked up the phone and spoke to his assistant. "See what you can dig up on Li Ming Chang."

A few minutes later, his assistant buzzed him. Michael picked up the phone. "Li Ming Chang is a Canadian citizen who has lived in Canada for five years. She is the CEO of a company called Friends of China Trading Company. There is not much on her LinkedIn profile or the Internet. The website is generic, with just a few pages. They only post an office address, phone number, and contact e-mail. On Facebook, she has posted many pictures and has over 1000 friends. Most of the pictures are of her with others. Some are pictures of her in a park or at the beach, others she appears to be at parties. There are some pictures of her with Jeremy and Iona. I suspect this was on their visit to Shanghai."

Michael thanked his assistant and hung up the phone. This all seemed innocent enough. Recently, Canada and China's diplomatic relations have been strained. That CSIS had taken an interest in Jeremy was significant. Michael performed a Google search. He found that CSIS was investigating prominent universities and their ties to China for medical research. The top university issued some guidelines to their researchers, suggesting they were not obligated to speak to the CSIS agents. Michael also reviewed a summary of China's involvement with Nortel. Nortel was Canada's leading telecommunication company. The military hacked into Nortel's computers and stole sensitive technology secrets. This hacking continued for the next ten years by the Internet company Huawei. Ultimately, Nortel went bankrupt because Huawei would constantly underbid them for contracts. Later, they determined that Nortel employees voluntarily gave much of the information to Huawei. The Chinese had recruited these employees to sell their secrets.

Michael did some research on proprietary medical information and China. There was not much. One article caught his attention. The success of controlling the COVID pandemic came from using mRNA vaccines. There was much interest in using similar technology for controlling cancers. Cancer-specific mRNA can boost immunity by producing specific proteins. The T cells produce antibodies that target proteins made by cancer cells for destruction. There was a tremendous amount of research involved in exploring this technology. Profits from drug companies would rise if cancer treatment centers used this developing technology.

This information did not seem relevant to Michael. Jeremy and Iona had been out of the country for the past year. They were not involved in cancer research. The most likely explanation for the CSIS interest in Jeremy was that they were seeking any information he might have. CSIS had targeted Li Ming Chang because her business had changed to medical conferencing. They suspected she was trying to recruit doctors and researchers to hand over proprietary medical research to the Chinese. CSIS was likely trying to determine whether Li Ming was recruiting Jeremy. Hopefully, Jeremy resolved that concern by speaking with them, as he had nothing proprietary to share.

Michael turned off his computer. His advice to Jeremy and Iona was simple. As they had done nothing wrong, they had nothing to fear from the spy agency. Something did not sit right with Michael. He could not put his finger on it but would remain vigilant in doing what he could to help Jeremy and Iona. He had become fond of them. They shared a history.

Chapter 3

Li Ming Chang was reading the latest report. The research had reached an impasse. The report suggested the scientists working on the project needed more samples. She had promised to provide more samples but had yet to deliver on the promise. They wrote the report in Mandarin. She was sitting at her desk in her condominium north of Toronto. Looking through her living room window, she could see in the distance the high-rise towers of Toronto lining the horizon. She thought about her situation. She needed those samples. Failure to get them was not an option. She thought about her parents and what she needed to do to protect them.

Li Ming Chang grew up as the only daughter. Li Ming Chang's parents raised her on a small farm. They had chickens and pigs and grew rice in a small terraced field. There was always enough for them to eat and any excess they sold at the local food market in the small village near their farm. Her parents were uneducated but believed that for Li Ming to survive in the modern world, she needed an excellent education. She was always the top student in her class. When she finished the equivalent of high school, her parents sent her to Fudan University in Shanghai. This C9 League university was one of the most prestigious universities in China. It was also one of the most difficult universities to gain admission to. With top marks throughout her schooling, this was an effortless task for Li Ming.

Li Ming was in her third year of a political science degree when she heard the news about her parents. High-speed train networks were being built across China. The project involved building railway lines through farmland. The farm where she grew up was smack in the middle of one of these proposed railway lines. When her parents objected and tried to organize a demonstration against this with the local farmers, they disappeared. Neighbors and friends cautioned her against asking too many questions and encouraged her to accept they were likely killed.

Li Ming had difficulty accepting their disappearance. Grieving privately, she was afraid that she, too, might become a target. When she asked the University for a compassionate 6-month leave from her studies, they denied it. She had trouble concentrating on her studies, and her grades were slipping. Crying herself to sleep every night made her constantly tired and depressed. She had no one to help her through this terrible time.

Sitting in the university cafeteria a month after her parent's disappearance, she was eating her lunch of noodles. A man wearing a business suit approached her. "May I sit down with you?" he asked politely. Li Ming noted he was in his mid-20s, a little older than she was. He wore glasses. There was a softness in his voice. He was handsome, wearing a well-fitting suit with a white shirt. He wore a bright blue tie with an expensive tie pin. His dark eyes fixated on hers with kindness.

"Feel free," she said.

He looked to the left and then to the right. There was no one within listening distance. He whispered in her ear, "My name is Huang Dong. I'd like to talk to you about your parents. Not here, though. We need to go somewhere more private, perhaps outside the park."

Li Ming stared at him in disbelief. She was immediately suspicious and fearful. He sensed it by saying, "Don't worry, I have good news. You are not in any danger. Come with me."

They both got up from the table. Li Ming left her half-finished bowl of noodles on the table. They walked outside across the street into the enormous park. There was an empty park bench where they both sat. "Your parents are alive," he said. When they tried to organize a protest against the high-speed railway being built through their farm, authorities arrested them. They had a quick trial and are in jail as dissidents. The courts convicted them of treason. They handed them 20-year sentences."

Li Ming burst into tears. The news that they were alive offered her renewed hope. The 20-year sentence for treason seemed unfair. They were unwitting peasants from the countryside, trying to scrape a living with what little they had. She was sobbing uncontrollably. Huang reached over and put his arm around her. Li Ming cried into his shoulder. When she could control her emotions and talk, she asked, "Why are you telling me this?"

"There is something you can do to help them," he said. "There's a way to get them out of prison. The government will find a new parcel of land for them. They will replenish the farm animals and give them enough land to grow rice."

"I will do anything!" cried Li Ming.

That is how Li Ming ended up in an apartment on the outskirts of Toronto. They recruited her five years ago. Li Ming's parents were happy on their farm, trying to make ends meet. They were oblivious to Li Ming's work. Nobody explained to them the reason for their release. Li Ming's mission was to infiltrate the medical research world in Toronto and send information back to China. The simple message given to her by these officials was if she failed, her parents would end up in jail.

Li Ming had made some progress by ingratiating contacts in the medical community with goodwill. She would organize medical conferences for Chinese doctors. Some of the invited speakers would be prominent Canadian physicians. She would pay them well for their 1-hour talk. Before the COVID pandemic, she would fly them and their wives to China in business class. She would have them speak at 5 or 6 hospitals. There would be accommodation in 5-star hotels. Chinese and Canadian guests would dine on the most exquisite Chinese cuisine every night. Guided tours also included famous sites in mainland China, such as The Great Wall, Terra Cotta Warriors of Xian, and the Yellow Mountain. The plan would be to gain their trust and encourage them to divulge research information useful to Chinese scientists.

Things had been going well until the embassy official explained CSIS had flagged her. Now, she was unsure what the future held. She would need to be very careful. Li Ming did not know how CSIS had found out about her mission, but the advice from the embassy was to avoid talking to them. CSIS agents were not the police. The embassy explained any discussion with the Canadian spy agency, CSIS, would need to be voluntary. Her instructions were explicit. Do not talk to them. So far, she had avoided them.

Chapter 4

Isabel, Iona's mother, lay on the hospital gurney in the pre-admission space of the hospital. The doctors planned to take Isabel to the operating room for the 6-hour surgery in 1 hour. She had carcinoma of the pancreas. The surgeon, Dr. Judy McLean, said she was lucky to have caught it early. "Most cancers of the pancreas are unresectable," she had explained at an earlier meeting. The surgical plan was to remove the head of the pancreas. It became a complex operation. The reconstruction of the gastrointestinal tract required surgeons with specialized training.

About one month earlier, she tripped over her golden lab while negotiating a visit to the washroom in the dark. She fell down some stairs after losing her balance. She lost consciousness and woke up after a few minutes. Slowly, she returned to the bedroom and called her daughter on her cell phone. It was 3 a.m.

Iona was asleep when she got the call. She had been in the Caribbean on her sailboat with her husband, Jeremy, for six months. They sailed to Grenada to avoid hurricane season and were at anchor.

"Hello," Iona said groggily.

"This is mom," said Isabel. "I just fell down some stairs after tripping over Lady. I think I hit my head and lost consciousness for a few minutes. I have pain in my tummy every time I take a deep breath. What should I do?"

By now, Iona was completely awake. She asked, "Do you feel lightheaded? What's your pulse rate? Call 911 and get an ambulance to take you to the hospital. Call me when you arrive, and let me speak to the emergency room doctor." Iona hung up the phone after Isabel agreed to call for an ambulance.

"What's the matter?" asked Jeremy, wide awake.

"Mom fell to the washroom and tripped over the dog. She thinks she lost consciousness for a few minutes. She has abdominal pain when she takes a deep breath. I told her to get an ambulance to the ER. She'll call when she sees the doctor," said Iona.

They both fell silent. Isabel lived by herself after her husband died in an accident ten years earlier. At 77 years old, she spent her days volunteering at the Metropolitan Hospital, where Jeremy used to work. She got by on her pension and a good pension left by her late husband. Isabel's determination to live alone concerned Jeremy and Iona. Over the past year, she seemed to lose her balance more often. Although she had never injured herself, they both felt she was at risk of injury. They would have to have another discussion with her when they returned to Toronto.

Jeremy got up and made coffee. Sleep would have to wait. Iona and Jeremy sat in the cockpit of their 51-foot boat. It was hot, and the air was thick with humidity. There was a gentle breeze from the ocean, which was refreshing. It was still dark outside, and cloud cover prevented the stars from shining through. Iona and Jeremy discussed her fall. They knew it would be a tough conversation to convince Isabel to enter an assisted living residence. It could wait until she got through this latest setback.

The phone rang. Iona answered, "Hello."

"Hi," said the voice at the other end of the phone. "I'm Dr. Gibson, the ER doctor looking after your mom. She gave me your number. She's fine now, and the abdominal pain she had when she got here is gone. We did a CAT scan of her head, chest, and abdomen. To my eyes, the CAT scan is normal, so that we will send her home. A radiologist will review the CAT scan in the morning."

"Great news!" exclaimed Iona. "Can I speak with her?"

"Hi honey," said Isabel. "The ER doctor is very nice. I feel much better, and my tummy pain is gone. The blood work is normal. The CAT scans are normal, so I will call a taxi to take me home. I'll call you later. I need some rest."

Iona hung up the phone and released a tremendous sigh of relief. Jeremy had opened the laptop and was banging away at the keyboard. "Jeremy, what are you doing?" asked Iona.

"I'm logging into Isabel's patient portal to look at the CAT scans myself," said Jeremy. Isabel had given him electronic permission to access her medical records a few years ago after her hip replacement. He clicked on the X-ray icon. From there, he found the CAT scans. Jeremy was the chief of surgery at the Metropolitan Hospital until ten months ago. A favorable, wrongful dismissal settlement from the hospital was generous. He had no incentive to work there again but respected many physicians and surgeons.

Jeremy first reviewed the head CAT scan. He admitted he was not an expert at reading 'heads' but could see no obvious abnormalities. The chest CAT scan looked normal as well. Jeremy had reviewed thousands of CAT scans of the abdomen during his career. The first thing he noticed was that all the abdominal organs were intact. There was no blood in the abdomen, excluding major damage from the fall. Jeremy systematically looked at the individual organs after a cursory look. The liver, spleen, kidneys, intestines, bladder, uterus, and ovaries looked normal. He focused on the pancreas. An obvious mass in the pancreatic head measuring 2 cm. in diameter. He could forgive the ER doctor for missing this because it was an incidental finding having nothing to do with her fall.

"Iona, have a look at this," said Jeremy. Iona sat down beside him. "I think there is a mass in the pancreatic head. It likely represents an early carcinoma. It is an incidental finding."

"Oh my God," said Iona. "Are you sure?"

"I'll call Jeff Maitland, the chief of radiology, in the morning and see what he thinks," said Jeremy.

Jeff Maitland confirmed the CAT scan finding. Isabel had carcinoma of the pancreas. There was no spread of the tumor, and it appeared resectable. Iona made plans to fly back to Toronto to support her mom and to drive her to the doctor's appointments. Jeremy agreed to stay behind and take care of the sailboat. Although they were south of the hurricane belt, storms still found their way to Grenada. If a storm came, Jeremy would find shelter at the Marina a few miles away.

Jeremy and Iona had been on their sailboat for the past six months. Anchoring in the bay gave them a freedom not experienced when living on land. There was always a gentle rocking, which helped with falling asleep. It was a beautiful way to spend time. In the Caribbean, the trade winds were a constant force, blowing from the east at 15 to 20 knots daily. The days blended into each other, as they were all the same. Brilliant sunshine, a gentle breeze, and happiness filled their days.

It took them the month of June to travel from the Dominican Republic to Grenada to avoid hurricane season, which lasts from June 1 to November 30 each year. Most of the hurricanes would appear in September and October. Usually, the hurricanes would not go further south than 12 degrees latitude, so they felt safe in Grenada at 10 degrees latitude. They made their days full by going to the local farmer's market every morning and getting fresh vegetables and fruit. They would hop in their dinghy and head to the beach. Often, they would run into other cruisers. They would discuss their plans for the day or discuss meeting for cocktails in the evening.

Leaving Jeremy and the simplicity of living on a sailboat was difficult for Iona. However, factors not within your control can sometimes change plans in life. Iona needed to be with her mother. It would be hard for her mother to get to the appointments alone. Her mother was always more worried about being a bother and would brush things off. Iona needed to be sure that she would get the best possible care.

Iona and Isabel met with the surgeon in her office. "It is rare for us to find cancer of the pancreas so early," said Judy McLean, the hepatobiliary surgeon assigned to her. "There is no spread of a tumor, and it appears resectable. Even in these early cases such as yours, the 5-year survival is only 16%. There is some good news, though. The tumor appears responsive in over 50% of cases to mRNA-induced immunotherapy. Some patients have a strong T cell immune response. They can generate antibodies to the tumor proteins and prevent cancer recurrence. It is experimental, but the early results are promising. We would need to test the immune response of your T cells. I would suggest we also get some blood samples from you, Iona. We have used T cells from a donor occasionally to help bolster the immune response."

The conversation continued for the next half an hour. Dr. McLean answered all their questions about the surgery and subsequent plans for mRNA immunotherapy. Iona and her mother went to the lab, and each gave about 20 vials of blood. It would take four weeks to get the results of the T cell response after the surgery. They would extract tumor cells from the specimen and send them to the lab. They would develop a vaccine specific to Isabel's cancer using mRNA technology. Dr. McLean explained pancreatic tumors create specific proteins. Antibodies created by the T cells against these proteins would prevent the spread of cancer. The key was to have high-functioning T cells capable of creating protein-specific antibodies.

When the day came for surgery, Isabel walked into the operating room with one of the OR nurses. All the preoperative workups had determined that Isabel was in excellent medical shape. The anesthesiologist found no health issues that would make the surgery more difficult. When she entered the operating room, they repeated the questions asked earlier. She lay on the operating table while the anesthesiologist hooked up the monitors. An OR nurse conducted a "time out" to confirm the correct patient and procedure. The last thing she remembered as she drifted off to sleep was the kind eyes of the OR nurse looking down at her while she was holding her hand.

Chapter 5

Bruce could hardly believe his eyes. He was looking at T cells that were functioning better than predicted. Bruce was a scientist at the University researching mRNA vaccines for cancer treatment. This new technology for treating cancers developed because of the success of COVID-19 vaccines. The concept was simple. Patients with cancer develop abnormal proteins attached to the tumor cells. The mRNA technology produced antibodies to destroy these abnormal proteins. This immune response would kill the tumor cells and cure the cancer patient.

Bruce knew that in science, things are not as simple as that, though. T cells are immunological cells that produce antibodies. Some patients had T cells that were better at producing antibodies than others. Those patients with higher functioning T cells responded better to this new cancer treatment. Bruce's research involved analyzing the ability of T cells to produce antibodies. The purpose was to stimulate the immune system so that everybody with cancer, even those with a weaker immune system, would have a cure.

Bruce was 41 years old. He had a PhD in immunology. Five years ago, they recruited him to work in the immunology research lab. He had thinning hair and a large bald area at the top. At 50 pounds overweight, he had developed a paunch resistant to gym exercise efforts. His thick glasses and poor eyesight prevented him from playing tennis and team sports. He had no interest in exercise, anyway. As long as he could remember, he would focus on tiny details. When he was little and saw a line of ants traveling in a straight line, he would lean down and watch them. Although his eyesight for distance was poor, he could see things clearly if they were close enough. He noticed that the ants' antennae would move back and forth. The antennae would pick up the pheromone signals from the others, which is how they communicated. These tiny details in life fascinated him.

Bruce grew up in a small town in southwestern Ontario. His parents both worked in the local automobile factory. Bruce was their only child. At four years old, his parents sent him for special testing. The doctors discovered he was on the autism spectrum. They were reluctant to label him with one of the syndromes because they discovered he had very high intelligence. However, he could not maintain eye contact and was slow to respond to verbal commands. When asked to color some pictures, he would become upset if the coloring pencils were not in the correct order in the box. During the testing, he threw the box of pencils on the floor, picked them up, and put them in the correct order.

Bruce often found that everyday conversation would create a great deal of effort. When asked, "How is your day going?" He would answer, "Mind your own business!"

He would become perplexed when they walked away in a huff. Not understanding their reactions, he tried different tactics. He simply stared at them when asked such mundane questions, not saying anything. When this resulted in a similar response, he tried shrugging his shoulders and avoiding eye contact. After a while, people would stop asking and give him the silent treatment. It, too, he found perplexing. Life was much simpler in the lab because scientific principles defined the process, logic, and the questions that needed to be asked.

The T cells he was testing belonged to a 77-year-old woman named Isabel. A few hours ago, the surgeons resected Isabel's carcinoma of the pancreas. Bruce was analyzing the samples. The T cells were called resident tissue T cells. As humans age, the quantity of circulating T cells diminishes, but the T cells in the tissue remain the same or increase. These resident tissue T cells would produce antibodies against the tumor-specific proteins. It would cause the tumor cells to implode and kill cancer. He knew this was the closest any scientist had come to curing cancer.

Bruce developed a method of extracting resident T cells from tissue. He had applied for a patent for this novel process and was waiting for the patent to be accepted. Once the patent came through, any laboratory that wanted to extract T cells to develop mRNA for cancer treatment would make huge profits. The patent would belong to the University. Any profits arising from the patented process would flow to the University. It would fund more scientific research. Bruce did the bulk of the current T cell research. He was having difficulty understanding why some profits would not flow to him. He had devoted his life to his work. It was unfair that he was getting a fixed salary that only allowed him to be slightly above the poverty line.

There were only a few research labs in the world that had the capabilities of T cell research. Bruce's work was further ahead than most in developing a cure for cancer. He had received discreet inquiries about whether he would consider working in other labs, but the University had him under a tight contract. He could not discuss his work with anyone. At staff meetings, there were discussions about this topic. Scientists at other institutions had faced criminal charges for leaking research information. It led to strict protocols and a code of conduct at Bruce's lab. When his contract was up, he would change jobs and only select laboratories that would share the profits with him.

Bruce was staring down at the lens of a microscope. He had never seen activity in producing antibodies as in Isabel's T cells. He had heard that some patients had increased T cell activity compared to others. No one had reported T cell activity to this extent. Isabel had a genetic propensity resulting in a hyper-functioning immune system. Bruce planned to keep this information and the details of her hyper immunity to himself for now. He would simply say that her T cells fell in the high-performance category.

He then turned to look at the blood sample that was drawn from her daughter, Iona. The circulating T cells were in abundance. They, too, were producing antibodies at a level he had never seen before. Bruce planned to study Iona's and Isabel's T cells in his spare time next month. He would work on a strategy to turn this into a profitable venture from which he would be the only one to benefit.

Chapter 6

When Isabel woke up, she recognized she was in the recovery room. Isabel volunteered at the hospital and frequently went to the recovery room to help. They had inserted an epidural catheter at the start of the surgery to help with the pain management. There was a large incision on her abdomen, but she had minor discomfort.

"Are you having any discomfort?" asked the recovery room nurse.

"I am very comfortable," answered Isabel. "I am taking deep breaths as instructed from my preoperative class, but I cannot wiggle my toes."

"That is because of the epidural catheter in your back, so don't worry about that. Dr. McLean told me that the surgery went as planned and there were no surprises. She will speak with you tomorrow when she sees you on her rounds," said the recovery room nurse.

They transported Isabel to her room after about an hour. Iona was waiting for her. Iona gently kissed her on her cheek. "You look amazing!" said Iona.

"I feel well, given that I've had my intestines rearranged and half my pancreas removed," responded Isabel. "I think this is the morphine talking."

"I spoke with Dr. McLean after the operation," said Iona. "Dr. McLean reported that there was no spread of the cancer, and she had completely removed it. However, she mentioned that the five-year survival rate, even in the best circumstances, is only 16%. The new mRNA vaccines against pancreatic cancers increase the 5-year survival to 60%. If you have high-performing T cells, the survival rates increase to 90%."

"Well, I'll keep my fingers crossed," said Isabel.

Dr. McLean visited Isabel at 8 a.m. on her morning rounds the following day. Iona had spent the night in Isabel's private room on a foldout bed. She had slept fitfully because of the noises that accompany a hospital stay. There was a code pink announced at 3 a.m. over the intercom, broadcasting the distress of a newborn in the labor and delivery suite. Iona could not sleep after that, so she went to the nursing station and chatted with the night nurses. The young night nurses were having a quiet night, and the 24 patients on the ward were all stable. The nurses were happy to talk about their kids and husbands. Two nurses at the desk planned to go on a holiday camping vacation together. It was a happy team of nurses on duty that night.

Iona went back to her foldout bed. Isabel had been sleeping like a rock all night. As there was nothing else to do, Iona drifted off to sleep around 6 a.m. She was still deep in her slumber when Dr. McLean entered the room. "My apologies for waking you two," she said.

"I wanted to share with you some great news," Isabel continued. "I spoke with Bruce, the lead scientist in the lab. He thinks Isabel will have a suitable response to the mRNA vaccine because she has high-performing tissue-resident T cells in her pancreas. It will take about one month to develop the tumor-specific cancer vaccine. She will be part of our study, but things look very optimistic about a cure."

"This sounds like the best scenario," said Iona.

"I doubt we will need any of your T cells, Iona," said Dr. McLean. "In some patients with poorly functioning T cells, we might use a compatible donor from a relative, but it will not be necessary in Isabel's case. We expect the mRNA vaccine Bruce develops to produce antibodies against the protein in the pancreatic cancer cells. It will cause the cancer cells to implode and prevent the cancer from spreading. We have never been so close to curing cancer."

"Thank you," said Isabel. "I appreciate everything you are doing for me."

"Let's get you through the post-op stage first," said Dr. McLean.

Six days later, they discharged Isabel from the hospital. Isabel insisted on going to her home but agreed to let Iona stay with her for a few days to help.

Iona called Jeremy. "Hi honey, we are at Mom's house, and everything is fine." They had a long discussion about Dr. McLean's optimistic outlook and shared their knowledge about the latest in immunotherapy.

"When are you coming back?" asked Jeremy.

"I think next week, if things continue to improve," said Iona. "Mom wants me to leave now, but I want to ensure she is strong enough. I'd like to return when she starts the immunotherapy to drive her to the appointments. That will be in about four weeks, so we should have a little time together in paradise before I leave again."

The following week, Iona flew back to Grenada.

Chapter 7

The warm trade winds filled in from the east. The gentle winds filled the sails as the *Iona Too,* their 51-foot sailboat, gracefully slid through the Caribbean Sea. It felt great to be on the move again, heading north now that hurricane season was almost over. Jeremy and Iona had hunkered down in Grenada below the hurricane belt. They stayed south to avoid the strong winds that could plague the northern Caribbean Islands in January. Now that February had arrived, it was safe to head north. As Iona was planning on helping her mother with doctors' appointments, they were heading for a Caribbean port close to an international airport. They selected Samana, Dominican Republic, because there were daily flights to Toronto. The plan involved Jeremy staying on the boat at the Puerto Bahia Marina while Iona could fly when her mother needed help.

The 600 nautical mile journey would take them four weeks, as they planned to stop along the way at some of their favorite spots. Bequia was one of the best islands in the Caribbean for sailors. Quiet anchorages surrounded by crystal blue waters. Admiralty Bay provided a great anchorage, protected from the ocean swells. There was spectacular snorkeling at the south end of the bay. There were two scuba shops where they could fill their tanks for deeper dives. The waters were warm and full of beautiful fish, colorful coral formations, and caves to explore. In the evening, the local restaurants served some of the best food on the windward islands. In short, there was nowhere better to spend time on the water.

The four weeks of perfect Caribbean weather flew by quickly. They stopped in Rodney's Bay, St Lucia, Jolly Harbor in Antigua, and then spent a few days anchored in Simpson's Bay in St. Martin. From there, they did the 2-day passage to Puerto Bahia Marina in Samana as *Iona Too* approached the Marina. Jeremy raised the harbor master on the VHF radio.

"Puerto Bahia Marina, Puerto Bahia Marina, Puerto Bahia Marina, this is Iona Too, Iona Too, Iona Too," said Jeremy into the radio.

"Jeremy, this is Gavin!" replied the voice on the radio. "Welcome back. It's great to hear your voice. We have you on dock C67, the same as last year, right in front of the hotel lobby."

"Great news," said Jeremy. "We'll be here at least a month, maybe longer."

Jeremy aimed the boat between the red and green channel markers and headed into the slip that was assigned to him. There were three marina staff on hand to help tie up *Iona Too* to the dock. After hooking the 50 Amp power cord to the electric outlet, they went to the customs office. There was a fee of $106.00 to pay for the cruising permit. The officer walked with them back to the boat and announced that he would like to do an inspection.

"No problem," said Jeremy.

"What do you think they are looking for?" asked Iona.

"Human smuggling is the main reason. Haiti is in such turmoil, so people will pay anything to escape," said Jeremy. "But they are always looking for drugs and other contraband."

"I wonder if they ever find human traffickers," pondered Iona. "What a terrible thought. I cannot think of anything more brutal. I have seen many patients that are victims of human trafficking."

Iona worked as a psychotherapist in Toronto. She had taken a year's leave of absence but was planning to return to work in May. Much of her practice of psychotherapy involved treating new immigrants to Canada. Many had been through terrible ordeals, and some were victims of human trafficking. Iona recalled Sophie, a 20-year-old woman from the Dominican Republic.

Jim and Marg McMillan, a couple from King City, a small town north of Toronto, had promised Sophie a job as a nanny. They had a 2-year-old boy who needed to be looked after while they went to work. At first, they seemed very nice. They gave Sophie her room and booked her into driving lessons. Once she knew how to drive, she could access the car on her days off. Before long, Jim started making suggestive comments about her figure. Sometimes, when he walked by, he would brush his body against her breasts. Marg and Jim entered her room one night and climbed into her bed. Jim held Sophie while Marg performed oral sex, and then they switched positions. Jim raped her while Marg held her down. They repeated these episodes every few days.

Marg and Jim warned her she was in Canada illegally and that any attempt to leave would cause her deportation back to the Dominican Republic. They had not applied for the right work visa to avoid paying taxes. It has saved them hundreds of dollars per month. Sophie was the middle daughter of seven children. She grew up in poverty in the Dominican Republic on a small farm. Although they often had enough to eat because they raised their chickens and cows, they left no money for anything else. It was the reason she came to Canada as a nanny. She realized Marg and Jim had tricked her into coming to Canada. Unless she did something, the abuse would go on indefinitely.

For all outsiders, the McMillans had a perfect family. A loving husband and wife were doting on their two-year-old son. One day, while cleaning the upstairs closet, Sophie came across an old video camera from the 1990s. It still worked. She set it up so they would not see it in her room. One night, when they visited her, she caught the entire episode on videotape. She made sure that she put up a stronger fight than usual so they could not claim the sexual abuse was consensual. The tape from the recorder was quite small and fit into her pocket without being noticed.

One of her duties during the day was to do the food shopping. Sometimes, she would run into her nanny friends. Often, they would talk about their employers. Until this point, she had said nothing about the sexual assaults because of her fear of getting deported. Today, she ran into Maya, a Filipino nanny working in Canada for two years. When Sophie saw Maya, she burst into tears.

"What's the matter, honey?" asked Maya.

Sophie just sobbed and sobbed. She was inconsolable. They stood just outside on the pavement in front of the grocery store. "Let's go grab a coffee in Starbucks," said Maya.

They both sat in a corner of Starbucks while Maya encouraged Sophie to talk. "Nothing can be so bad that you cannot share with a friend. I've been through a few rough times myself. It's always good to talk about tough times."

"I can't tell you," said Sophie. "If I do and they find out, they will deport me back to the Dominican Republic, and I'll never be able to come back."

"Wow!" exclaimed Maya. "You are in Canada now. Despite being on temporary visas, we expect to be treated appropriately as we have rights. Just by telling you they will have you deported, they are violating your human rights. I'm not letting you out of here until you tell me what's happening."

Sophie told her about the bedroom visits. She told Maya about the videotape. Sophie did not know what she should do with it. Now, she was worried that Maya might get in trouble as well. She felt even worse.

"I have the beginnings of a plan," said Sophie. "When I first came to Canada, I had a lot of emotional difficulties being so far away from the Philippines. I met with a doctor called Iona Young. She was amazing. Not only did she support me, but she taught me ways to cope. I have never been happier. I have reduced my visits to once a month, but I am meeting with her tomorrow. Give me the tape, and I will show it to her. She will know what to do."

Sophie reached down into her pocket and pulled out the tape. She gave it to Maya reluctantly. "Meet me back here tomorrow after work," said Maya.

When Sophie returned to the house, Marg and Jim were waiting for her. "What kept you so long," said Jim.

"I ran another nanny, and we went for coffee," said Sophie.

"You little bitch," screamed Marg. "You use our car. We pay for your upkeep. We feed you. All we ask is that you respect us. Going for coffee without our permission is disrespectful. It must never happen again. Got it?"

Jim wound up his right arm and made a fist. He balanced all his weight onto his right foot and let loose a powerful punch. It caught Sophie on the right side of her face, causing her neck to bend almost 90 degrees. The bags of food she was carrying went flying against the wall. Crumpled on the floor, she hit her head on the hard marble tile. She felt dazed. She recollected being taken to her bedroom, where they both took turns assaulting her sexually. Not sleeping a wink that night, she realized it was just a matter of time before they killed her.

While Marg and Jim went to work the next day, Sophie cared for their son. At around 4:00 p.m., she fed him and then put him to bed for his afternoon nap. They would come home at around 5:00 p.m. She left the house shortly before five and walked to the Starbucks, about two miles away. Sophie had to wear dark glasses because she had raccoon eyes from the beating. She sat quietly in the corner, praying that Marg and Jim would not discover her. Shortly after 7:00 p.m., Maya walked in. She sat down beside Sophie, and they both burst into tears. "Oh my God!" cried Maya. "You can never go back there. They will kill you."

Sophie wept. She did not know what to do next. Maya pulled her close and let her cry while resting her head on her shoulder. "Come with me," she whispered. "There's someone I would like you to meet."

Iona was waiting for them in the car. She had dealt with similar cases of abused victims of human trafficking before. They drove to the hospital, where Sophie underwent a complete examination, including a rape test. The rape test confirmed sexual assault. There were tears in her vagina. They collected the semen and bagged it for later use in criminal proceedings. The CAT scan of her head, chest, and abdomen showed no major injuries. As it was late at night, Iona brought her to her house, where she stayed in the spare room and would be safe. The next day, she visited an immigration and a criminal lawyer. They took her to the police station, where she filed charges.

They sentenced Marg and Jim McMillan to ten years for unlawful confinement, assault, and rape. It took two years of intensive psychotherapy with Iona for Sophie to feel safe. The officials at Immigration Canada granted Sophie landed immigrant status because of her ordeal. Sophie went to college to learn computer programming. She landed a job with one of the big banks when she got her degree. She felt indebted to Iona for saving her life.

Reflecting on Sophie's story, Jeremy and Iona had no problem allowing the immigration officials to inspect their boat. Looking for human smugglers was a needed endeavor.

Chapter 8

For sailors, Puerto Bahia Marina was a dream come true. Jeremy and Iona docked ***Iona Too*** in front of the 5-star hotel's open lobby. They had access to the restaurants, the tennis courts, the exercise gym, and, best of all, the Infinity swimming pools. The sailors would arrive planning on spending a day or two on their way either north to the Bahamas or south to the Caribbean islands. Invariably, they would spend a month or longer in this paradise. At the end of each glorious day, the sailors would meet at the Ocean View Restaurant for cocktails and to watch the sunset. The sunsets were spectacular. The sailors spent many evenings telling sailing stories about adventures at sea. They discussed the exotic, distant lands that they had visited. Everyone would listen attentively as the stories got wilder and more exciting. They would advise on the best places to anchor at a particular location. Others would warn about which islands to avoid and which were a must-visit. They developed strong friendships, knowing they may never see each other when they took off for distant lands. It was the sailing community and their shared experiences that drew them together.

Jeremy would take the dinghy to the nearby town's fresh fruit and vegetable market every few days. It was mango season, and they were practically giving them away. Papayas and other fruits tasted out of this world. The organically grown vegetables were free of chemicals. They were delicious. There was always fresh fish caught during the night by the local fishermen.

The weather was perfect. It was warm during the day and evening, just cool enough for a restful sleep. When it did rain, it would only pour for 15 minutes and then stop. The jungle was lush, and the vegetation was a deep green. The gardeners of the Marina were always in a constant battle with the jungle to prevent it from taking over the property.

Every morning, Jeremy would go for a 10-kilometer run along the road. A well-worn footpath along the side of the road afforded a degree of safety from the speeding trucks and motorcycles. He would try to finish the run before it got too hot. In the afternoon, while sitting in the cockpit, the sailors would drop by, and they would talk. The conversation would drift from weather discussions to sailing destinations. It was a wonderful way to spend the day. Iona had flown back to Toronto to help drive her mother to doctors' appointments. She wanted to be available to help with her chemotherapy in case there were difficulties. Jeremy remained in the Dominican Republic to look after the boat and do maintenance and repairs. He hoped Iona would be back within a few weeks.

Such was life in the tropics, savoring the beauty, warmth, and freedom of worry.

Jeremy was sitting in his cockpit reading. It was about 5:30 in the evening, almost time to watch the sunset from Ocean View restaurant. "Hi there," said a familiar voice from the dock. It was Judy and her sailing friend Wendy. "We're on our way to watch the sunset. Do you want to tag along?"

Judy and her husband David had arrived by power boat from Punta Cana 3 weeks ago. They were on their way to the Bahamas. They planned to spend a month at the Marina. David had flown to Washington a week ago for business but was returning to the Marina the following day. Judy and David would leave for the Bahamas in the next weather window, which appeared to be within a few days. All sailors ever talked about were their plans. Everybody within earshot knew what each other was going to do. However, with sailing, plans change with the weather or, more often, for no good reason.

"I was just heading there myself," said Jeremy. "I'd love to tag along."

The two women were in a very pleasant mood. It was clear to Jeremy they had been drinking before leaving their boat. "We had ourselves a few cocktails on my boat before we left," giggled Wendy. "My husband, Joe, passed out, so we girls will have a good time tonight. Whoo Hoo!"

At least twenty other sailors, mostly couples, sat on the lawn outside the Ocean View Restaurant. They were drinking cocktails and getting ready to watch the sunset. It was spectacular. A green flash appeared for one second the moment the sun disappeared. All the sailors watching the show began hooting and hollering. "We're all going to get laid tonight!" shouted Wendy.

"That's the first time I've seen the green flash!" whispered Judy into Jeremy's ear. "I'm so glad David's not here!"

Only after the sun went down did the spectacular light show begin. The entire horizon lit up in pink, purple, and orange, reflecting on the low-hanging clouds. The colors spread across the sky from horizon to horizon. There were cheers from the sailors delighting in the show. When darkness set in after 15 minutes, the sailors settled on their lawn chairs and began telling their stories.

Jeremy sat in a chair, finishing his beer. The light show had been spectacular, but he planned to return to the boat for an early night. He was going to do a 10-kilometer run in the morning but wanted to start before it got too hot. It meant getting up at 6:00 a.m. Judy sat down beside him. They started talking. Jeremy talked about Iona and how she was taking care of her mother while she went to chemotherapy appointments. Judy talked about David.

"David says he's gone to Washington for business," said Judy. "Last time he went for business, I hired a private detective. It turns out he has a 25-year-old girlfriend. For a week, he never left her apartment. They lived on Uber Eats and each other. You do not know how pissed off I am. We've been married for 25 years, and I've had no relations outside of the marriage. That is about to change tonight. Jeremy, I want to fuck you."

Jeremy had just taken a swig of beer, and Judy's proposition caused him to choke. A stream of beer left his esophagus and spewed out onto the lawn. He was having trouble breathing. Judy laughed so loud that others stopped to see what was funny.

When Jeremy finally got himself together, he said, "Judy, that's not going to happen. I have a great relationship with my wife and would do nothing like that. I miss her terribly. Every day, I speak with her on the phone. I am looking forward to when she comes back with me. She'll be back here in about two weeks. I'm sorry you are so unhappy, but I can't help. I'm heading back to my boat now. I suggest you go back to your boat before you do something you regret."

With that, Jeremy stood up and walked away without giving her a chance to respond. He returned to his boat, brushed his teeth, and crawled into bed. The conversation troubled him. He would need to consider whether he did or said something that might have made her think he was interested in her. He drifted off into a fitful sleep.

It was pitch black in the stateroom. Jeremy was wide awake. Judy had crawled into bed with him and was naked. She was slurring her speech, describing what she would do to him. Suddenly, she vomited. A huge liquid bile-stained river splashed over Jeremy and the bed. She began to cry and was sobbing uncontrollably. Within the next 30 seconds, she was fast asleep.

Jeremy leaped up from the bed and put the lights on. He stared down at the mess of vomitus that soaked into the bedsheets. Judy's naked body lay in a vomit-free area. Jeremy grabbed an extra blanket and put it over top of her. Jeremy went to the bedroom on the port side at the back of the boat, took a quick shower to wash off the chunks of vomit on his chest, locked the door, and crawled into bed. Sleep did not arrive until it got light. When he got up, it was 8:00 a.m. He unlocked his bedroom door and went to his bedroom. All that was remaining of Judy was the imprint of where she had slept and her partially dried vomit. She was gone.

Jeremy spent the rest of the day cleaning up the boat. A washing machine was on board, and he washed all the sheets. He scrubbed and cleaned the mattress, attempting to eliminate the smell. He would need to tell Iona about what happened. It would need to be in person. He briefly contemplated returning to Toronto, but she would return in about two weeks. He expected it would be a tough conversation, as this was a sensitive topic for Iona.

Jeremy thought back to when he was to receive an award at the hospital. It was several years ago. The award was to be presented to him at the annual gala. Before dinner, Iona and Jeremy were standing in the lobby sipping on a glass of champagne. A woman he barely knew but worked at the same hospital joined them.

She said in a sultry voice, "Iona, you are so lucky to have such a sexy man. If you ever get sick of him, let me know, and I'll take him in a flash."

She then attempted to kiss him on the lips. Jeremy turned his head at the last minute, and she kissed his ear. The woman turned on her heels and sped away.

"What the hell was that about, Jeremy?" said Iona loudly.

"I have no idea, Iona. I don't even know her name. I know she works in the hospital's finance department, but I have absolutely no clue where that came from," said Jeremy.

"These behaviors don't typically happen out of the blue. You must have had some interaction with her," said Iona.

"Iona, I'm drawing a blank here," said Jeremy.

Iona was frosty towards Jeremy the rest of the evening. When Jeremy received his award, he carefully thanked his wife, Iona, for providing such a supportive environment. In the car on the way home, Iona said, "We've been married 25 years. You do not know about a woman's intuition when picking up infidelity. We women sense things that you men cannot. If you ever had an affair or even had a fleeting thought about it, I would know about it. I would drop you like a stone. I told you that when we married, and I'm telling you again now, 25 years later."

"Understood," said Jeremy. "You never have to worry about anything like that because it has never happened, and it will never happen."

Jeremy knew he would have to choose his words carefully when he talked with Iona about what had happened with Judy. He was not looking forward to that conversation.

Chapter 9

Bruce was lying in bed beside the most exquisite woman in the world. She breathed softly in a deep sleep while her head rested on his bare chest. He gently ran his fingers through her thick black hair in awe of her beauty. She seemed to find his ineptitude with social interactions delightful. Nobody had ever paid much attention to him. He knew from a very early age that he differed from everyone else. Bruce didn't understand why, but girls never found him attractive. He had never been on a date during his 40 years on Earth until he met Mi Ling.

About six months ago, the laboratory director invited Li Ming to tour the laboratory facility. She represented a large Chinese conglomerate offering an unlimited grant to help with their research. From the moment he saw her, she captivated him. The graceful way she would glide across the room and enter his personal space made him weak at the knees. Bruce could smell lilacs in her perfume. She greeted him with a smile and held his hand. Her hand was warm and soft. Her dark eyes focused on him. She seemed fascinated by his work. Because of the sensitive nature of the research, he could only discuss the research in general terms. As he was talking with her, she would sometimes touch his arm, which would send electric shocks to the core of his body. She looked at him like he was the most handsome, smartest, and most desirable man in the world. He had encountered no one like Mi Ling.

Bruce found himself unable to stop thinking about Li Ming after she left the laboratory facility following the 1-hour tour. He recognized he was so socially handicapped he could not approach her and ask her for a date. He could not sleep because she occupied his thoughts. Bruce knew his research was suffering because he could not focus. All he could think about was that last image of Li Ming. She touched his face while her dark eyes softly looked into his. That image remained etched in his brain.

A month later, as he was staring down at a microscope, his phone rang at around 2:00 p.m. Annoyed as it interrupted his work, he briefly contemplated not answering it. Bruce suspected it was from his boss. On at least three occasions, when it rang, his boss had given him explicit instructions to answer his phone.

"Hello," said Bruce.

"Hi Bruce, this is Li Ming. We met when I did a tour of your laboratory," said the voice at the other end of the line. "Do you remember me?"

Bruce's hand holding the phone trembled. Within 2 seconds, his entire arm shook with such ferocity that the phone flew out of his hand and across the room. It violently darted back into the desk, attached by the cord, and smashed into pieces. He could still hear Li Ming's voice through the small speaker lying on the floor, no longer housed in the protective plastic casing. "Hello Bruce? Are you OK? Are you there?"

All Bruce could do was stare at the broken pieces of the phone. He opened his mouth to speak, but no words came out. He had been in trouble before for breaking a phone when he did not like how the conversation was going. They deducted the cost of repairs from his pay. This was different. He did not know what to do or what to say. After a minute, it was as though Li Ming had given up on him and stopped asking about him. The speaker went silent.

Bruce sat down at the desk and pushed his head in his hands. How could he be so inept? The woman occupying his thoughts had called him. Bruce knew he might never have the opportunity to speak with her again. He was kicking himself silently, extremely disappointed in himself. He did not know how long he was sitting there when someone tapped him on the shoulder after what might have been 15 minutes. It was the security guard from the front desk.

"Someone dropped this off for you," he said. The security guard handed Bruce an envelope with his name on it.

Bruce immediately tore open the envelope. "Meet me at the Starbucks on Bay and Bloor at 5 p.m.." was all it said. The beautifully constructed cursive note smelled of lilac perfume.

That was six months ago. Since then, his life has radically changed. Even his coworkers noticed the change. He seemed less sarcastic and more helpful. At the weekly research meetings, he would answer troublesome questions about their work collectively. This changed from his usual response to remaining silent during these meetings. However, the biggest change for Bruce was a renewed enthusiasm for his research. Li Ming seemed obsessed with his work on T cells. She was exceptionally bright and understood the concepts better than many researchers he worked with. Her interest in his work sped up his thought process. He was looking for ways of impressing her with his new processes.

There were many things that Bruce knew about T cells that no one else in the world knew. For example, he could extract T cells from human tissue. He had developed techniques for determining whether these T cells could produce antibodies to fight cancer. No one else in the world had developed this technology. Last night, he told her about his latest finding, super-functioning T cells. They were lying in bed when she lay on top of him and started rubbing herself against him. After they had finished, she rolled off him, curled against him, and, within a minute, was snoring softly. Bruce fell into a peaceful sleep. He had never experienced passion or ecstasy until he met Mi Ling. He was unsure he knew what love was, but he was certain this was the closest he would ever get to it.

Bruce and Li Ming were sitting at her breakfast table. They had just finished eating their omelets and were drinking coffee.

"I started telling you about super-functioning T cells last night," said Bruce.

"All I remember about last night was you bringing me to orgasm three times," whispered Li Ming. "You were amazing."

Bruce opened his mouth to speak, but nothing came out. When Li Ming spoke crudely to him, it was as if his body had stopped functioning. She laughed softly and put her index finger on his mouth. "You are very special," she said. "I want to hear all about it."

Bruce sipped his hot coffee to clear his thoughts and told her about Isabel's super-functioning T cells. "She has pancreatic cancer, and I have no doubt the mRNA vaccine that we give her will prevent the cancer from ever coming back."

Li Ming stared at Bruce. "Is this different from other patients?' asked Li Ming

Bruce answered, "Broadly speaking, the cancer patients fall into two major categories. Those with T cells that are capable of producing antibodies against their cancer, and those patients who cannot. It is unclear why there is a difference, but I continue investigating it. I am keeping these results secret because I believe I will find a cure for cancer and one day will sell it to the highest bidder.

"I am only partly serious about making a fortune. If the lab discovers what I am doing, they will claim ownership of the technology. I have yet to work out the details, so I get to keep all the benefits of my work.

"In the meantime, I keep working away. An interesting thing I identified was that her daughter also has super-functioning circulating T cells. I suspect the two have a genetic predisposition to produce these T cells."

Li Ming said, "You once explained that T cells originate in the neonatal thymus gland. Because the body has not exposed the T cells to any pathogens, they have produced no antibodies. Shouldn't we look for T cells that have encountered no pathogens? That way, there would be a maximum response to antibody production. Infants get deathly sick when they get a cold but bounce back quickly. You told me this is likely because of the intense antibody production in these hyper-functioning young T cells. The older we get, the slower the T cells function."

"You are correct," said Bruce. "That is one theory why cancer is more common in older adults. We have discussed the topic you mentioned in immunotherapy meetings across the world. The problem comes in obtaining neonatal thymus glands. It would be unethical to extract thymus tissue from newborn infants. One option would be to perform in vitro fertilization for the sole purpose of extracting thymus tissue. The thymus gland reaches development at approximately nine weeks of gestation. They would destroy the embryo afterward. They have banned this kind of research. Anyone contemplating doing this would need to understand they might spend the rest of their lives in jail."

Bruce had never discussed these topics like this with anyone else. He found that most would simply not understand what he was talking about, and he did not have the patience to explain. His work fascinated Li Ming. This drove him to perform at an even higher level. He had met no one interested in the same things he was. For Bruce, life had taken on a larger meaning. With Li Ming by his side, he was bound to perform extraordinary things.

After Bruce left for work that morning, Li Ming drove to the Chinese Embassy in Toronto. She walked past the security after showing her identity card. She went to the 2nd floor and entered an office marked 'private.' A red phone rested in the middle of a small desk. She sat on the office chair. The phone was secure, and no one could trace conversations. She dialed the number she had committed to memory.

Chapter 10

Jeremy and Iona were sitting at the Ocean View restaurant at the Puerto Bahia Marina, about to watch the sunset. Iona had arrived from Toronto about a week earlier after having spent one month helping her mother to the chemotherapy appointments. They planned to sail back to Toronto in the next weather window. They would sail to New York City, motor up the Hudson River, go through the Erie Canal system to Oswego, New York, and then sail across the lake to Toronto. The trip would take about three weeks. They had hired a weather router, Casey Perkins, to get the best departure advice. The email he sent them this morning said there was a fast-moving tropical wave heading their way that would bring bad weather. He recommended allowing this to pass before heading off. This would mean a few more days in paradise before they could leave.

The sun disappeared over the horizon as they sat on the lawn, watching the sunset with the other sailors. There was a green flash. It happened in less than a second. Iona grabbed Jeremy's hand. She planted a long kiss on his lips. She looked at him and said, "It's great to be here with you."

Jeremy's memory drifted back to when he last saw the green flash. He had not yet told Iona about that incident involving Judy. There never seemed to be a good time. Iona picked up on Jeremy's discomfort.

"What's the matter, honey?" Iona said.

"There's something I need to discuss with you, " Jeremy said. "About three weeks ago……."

The conversation was interrupted by Jeremy's phone ringing. "Hello," he said.

"Hi Jeremy, this is Casey. This morning, I emailed you about a tropical wave moving quickly toward you. That tropical wave has stalled, and I think a weather window has opened for tomorrow. You would have consistent trade winds from the east for the next four days that would get you north of 26 degrees latitude. Likely, you would have a day or two of motoring before picking up the northeast winds. The forecast can only be accurate for five days, and it will take eight days to get to New York City by my calculation. I will contact you in four days to update you on the last leg of your trip."

"Great news!" said Jeremy. "I have Starlink, so that I will download the daily weather forecasts."

There was further discussion about wind direction and wind strength. The conversation ended with Casey promising to update the weather forecast in four days.

Jeremy and Iona walked back to the boat. They talked about last-minute preparations they needed to do before leaving at sunrise. Stopping at the immigration office, they informed them they would leave in the morning. The passports got stamped, and the boat papers signed. Jeremy checked the oil level on the engine and generator. They were both fine. They both walked around the boat, securing the life raft and their dinghy. It was about 9:00 a.m when they were sitting in the cockpit trying to think of anything else they needed to do when Judy walked by with her husband, David.

"Jeremy, nice to see you! We're trying to avoid that tropical wave coming our way, but we just found out that it stalled," said Judy. She was slurring her speech. Jeremy recognized she had been drinking. Jeremy dreaded what might come next.

"We'll stay here tonight," said David, trying to control the conversation. "Then we'll take off first thing in the morning. Judy, let's get to customs and immigration before they close."

"Not so fast, David. While you were fucking your 25-year-old tart in Washington, I spent the night on this boat with Jeremy," slurred Judy. "We had a great time, didn't we, Jeremy?"

David glared at Judy. Then he glared at Jeremy. "You asshole," he shouted at Jeremy. "Let's get away from these freaks." David grabbed Judy and started dragging her towards the immigration office.

Judy started laughing, pleased that she had elicited a response from David. Jeremy could hear her laughing as she continued down the dock. When Jeremy looked from where Iona had been sitting, she was no longer there. He heard the aft cabin door slam and then lock.

"Iona," said Jeremy softly, trying to talk through the locked door. "We need to talk."

"You have had over a week to talk to me, and you mentioned nothing," said Iona. "Why would I want to talk with you now?"

Jeremy knew it was useless to persist. He could only hope that she might have settled down in the morning. Jeremy made his way to the main bedroom and lay down. It astonished Jeremy how quickly things could go south with a relationship as strong as theirs. He must have drifted off to sleep around 2:00 in the morning. He awoke poorly rested at 6 a.m. when the alarm went off. The door to the aft cabin remained locked. He could see through the cockpit window Iona's legs, so he knew she was still there.

Jeremy started the engine. He released the mooring lines and threw them on the boat. He used his bow thruster to aim the boat into the channel. Once clear of the Marina, he fastened himself onto the jack lines using his life jacket tether. Iona and Jeremy had made up a list of safety maneuvers, and connecting to the jack lines at all times was one of them. Another safety rule was not going onto the foredeck without backup in the cockpit. However, Iona was still not talking to him. He needed to stow the fenders and secure the mooring lines before they got washed overboard with the waves. Jeremy fastened himself to the jack line, running up and down the boat's length, and completed the task.

It was a 15-mile voyage to the entrance of the Bay of Samana, directly into the easterly trade winds. Jeremy motored 2 hours before he could clear the cape. Upon clearing the cape, Jeremy hoisted the mainsail and set the jib. He set the auto helm for a direct route to New York City, 1500 miles away. Jeremy turned off the engine. The trade winds were at right angles to the direction where the boat was heading. This was the fastest and most comfortable point of sail for *Iona Too*. She caught the wind and glided through the water like a thoroughbred horse at the racetrack. It was beautiful. The motion through the water was gentle and comforting.

Jeremy set the alarms so that if another boat came within one nautical mile, it would alert him. He then lay on the cockpit cushions and drifted off to sleep. When he woke up two hours later, Iona was behind the steering wheel, looking at the chart plotter.

"I'm not ready to talk if you're wondering," said Iona. "We agreed we would do three-hour shifts. My shift started an hour ago. I would appreciate it if you stayed out of my space while I am on my shift."

Jeremy went below deck and made a sandwich. Iona did not respond when he asked her if she wanted one. It was going to be a long, painful voyage, he thought.

Chapter 11

The surgeon made a tiny incision in the right groin. Cautery dealt with any small amount of bleeding. He carried the dissection down to the inguinal canal. Using his gloved index finger, he encircled the spermatic cord. He gently pulled the testicle out of the scrotum and into the operative field. Using hemostatic clamps, he divided the spermatic cord. He sutured either end with surgical ties. He then handed the testicle off to a waiting team member. Using calipers, he measured the dimensions of the testicle to be 45 mm X 25 mm X 28mm. His assistant opened a sterile case containing different-sized prosthetic Silastic testicles. He chose one of the same dimensions and slid it into the empty hemi-scrotum. Then, he sutured the skin with dissolving sutures and used glue to pull the wound together. The entire operation took less than 10 minutes.

The waiting team packed the testicle on ice and sent it to the laboratory in an ambulance. Using lights and sirens, they reduced the trip time to 3 minutes. The researchers were waiting at the door. They received the specimen in less than 8 minutes from the time the surgeon removed the testicle. Plastic tubing was used to cannulate the testicular artery and vein. They perfused the blood vessels to the testicle with perfluorocarbon emulsion. This solution carries more oxygen than natural hemoglobin. A warm-saline solution bath housed the testicle at 36 degrees, 1 degree lower than the usual body temperature of 37 degrees. This allowed the testicle to function in the most natural environment. The testicle was now ready.

Wang could not believe his luck. He was sitting on the high-speed train from Xian to Shanghai. The 1500-kilometer trip would only take 6 hours. He was 16 years old, early in high school in Xian. He had never been on the train before. It was going 300 kilometers an hour. Fields and houses sped by the window so quickly he could barely see them. The train ride was smooth. The train's speed was lit up in neon red at the front of the cabin. 314 kilometers per hour! And to think his parents did not want him to go.

There was a notice posted in his school about a research experiment. They needed blood from young, healthy males. Each participant would get paid 100 Yuan, but they would draw for a larger prize from all 2000 participants. Wang had been the winner. The trip included an all-expense paid weekend to Shanghai with a visit to the nightclub *M1nt.* This is one of Shanghai's most popular nightclubs, on the top (24th) floor of a Nanjing Road East skyscraper. Although he was too young to drink alcohol, many young people went there. They assured him there would be some famous movie stars and it would be a night to remember. They had reserved a room for him at the Waldorf Astoria Shanghai on the Bund. His friends were all jealous of his good luck.

A beautiful Chinese woman named Li Ming accompanied him. She had been the one organizing the participants for the research. She had assured Wang's parents that they would take good care of him. Upon arriving at the train station in Shanghai at around 3:00 p.m., two other research team members welcomed them. They took Wang to the hotel for a rest before they met for dinner at 8 p.m. The dinner was amazing. There was a group of eight of them sitting around a table. The servers placed the food in the center, which would rotate for the guests so they could choose whatever they wished to eat. There was fresh fish, rice, and some delicious food he had never seen before.

After dinner, they went to the **M1nt** nightclub on the top floor of the high-rise. The view was spectacular. Shanghai was lit up with bright neon lights. He was drinking virgin margaritas while the rest of the team, who were adults, were drinking the real thing. He remembers dancing with Li Ming and watching as the clock turned midnight. The last thing he remembers was feeling tired and sitting at the table. He tried to keep his eyes open, but he felt himself slipping down a dark hole as slumber overtook his body.

Wang woke up, not knowing where he was. He looked around the room. It was a beautiful, expensive hotel room. He had a dull ache in his right groin and noticed when he went to urinate, there was a tiny cut there. He did not recall injuring himself. Wang could not recall much about the previous night. He remembered winning the prize and the amazing high-speed train ride. There was a knock on his door.

"You must get ready," said the voice. "We must be at the train station by noon. How are you feeling?" It sounded like Li Ming. Wang opened the door.

"Give me 5 minutes to get my things together," said Wang. "I feel a little foggy this morning. I can't remember much about last night."

"You fell on the dance floor and cut yourself on a piece of glass. We had to take you to the hospital for stitches," said Li Ming. "You don't remember?"

"What are you talking about?" asked Wang. "No way, I don't remember anything like that."

"There was only a minor cut. The doctor was not even sure he should stitch it but did this partly because we were going on a long train ride this afternoon. Have you seen that tiny cut?" asked Li Ming.

"I was wondering how it got there," said Wang. "Now it makes sense. Can we keep this quiet from my parents?"

"We can talk about that later," said Li Ming. "I'll meet you in the lobby in 5 minutes."

Li Ming accompanied Wang back to Xian on the high-speed train. She smiled to herself, thinking how easy it was. They identified Wang as having very high-functioning T cells in his blood sample. Now they had his testicle and could extract sperm. They needed to find a female with similar high-functioning T cells. They could then extract her ovum and perform in vitro fertilization.

Once the embryo grew to 9 weeks they would extract high functioning T cells from the thymus. Using mRNA technology, they would then use these high functioning T cells to produce antibodies against the cancer. It was going to make them rich. People with cancer would pay enormous sums of money to be cured.

After dropping off Wang at his home in Xian, Li Ming caught a flight to Beijing. She connected to an Air Canada flight, which took her to Toronto. Her next task would be to find that woman.

Chapter 12

They had been at sea for three days. The trade winds remained strong on the beam for the entire time. *Iona Too* loved this point of sail and flew along at 9 knots. They had already knocked off 600 nautical miles of the 1500 to New York City. The sun was shining, and there were no clouds in the sky. The strong breeze, although warm, was refreshing against their skin. A cockpit covered with the bimini and dodger protected them from the tropical sun and kept them cool. Iona and Jeremy had fallen into a routine of three-hour watches. Their sailing routine was to always have someone on watch in the cockpit. That person could nap for 30 minutes if they set the alarms. Thirty minutes was the time it took for a ship traveling at 20 knots to reach them when first spotted on the horizon. There were few commercial vessels in the middle of the Bermuda Triangle where they traversed. The chart plotter shows no vessels in the visual range.

Jeremy was finishing his 4 AM-7 AM three-hour shift. He was looking forward to a luxurious 3-hour nap before his next shift. Iona appeared in the cockpit, carrying 2 cups of coffee. "I am ready to talk," she said.

Jeremy then explained the story about Judy and how she ended up on their boat. He said, "You once explained that these things just do not happen out of the blue. Very often, some things might have occurred that would precipitate this kind of behavior. I can't recall anything that happened between Judy and me, which could have given the impression that I was remotely interested in her."

"Let me explain something else then," said Iona. "I have been doing psychotherapy for the last 25 years. My patients tell me I have amazing intuition. They have mentioned that I'm almost psychic. Sometimes, I can diagnose their psychiatric condition the moment they walk in the door. Understanding why I am so good at this took me a while. The best way to explain it would be to look at basic animal behavior. If an aggressive dog approaches a human, the dog might attack that human. With other humans, the same aggressive dog might just roll onto the back and expose their belly in an act of contrition. Ever wonder why?"

"I always assumed that they could smell fear," said Jeremy. "Fear makes them angry and aggressive. Another possibility is that their body language shows fearfulness, making them a target."

Iona stated, "I think they can smell anxiety. When humans feel anxious, they release pheromones that smell like a wet brown paper bag to me. A patient coming into my office with either depression or anxiety excretes these pheromones. It took me a while to learn how to control my emotions because this smell also elicits a chemical response in my body that makes me angry. Like the dogs that have an overwhelming urge to attack a frightened human, I feel the same way when I smell anxiety or depression. Over the years, I have learned to control this anger so I do not make their anxiety worse.

"When Judy walked up to us that night, although she was drunk, the alcohol could not mask the wet paper bag smell that drifted over our boat. That was what made me uncontrollably angry. Not only was I upset that you had not discussed this with me ahead of time, but my physiological response also resulted in anger. I suspect she is suffering from a terrible depression besides anxiety. The moment of pleasure she got from her husband's sharp response would only be short-lived."

Jeremy thought about this for a moment. He thought back to a time when he had terrible anxiety. During his surgery training, he was studying for his surgery exams. The exams had a reputation of being extremely tough, and there was a failure rate of at least 50%. He remembered a time when Iona was especially angry with him. His exams were the following day. It was late at night, and he was pacing the floor. Iona was livid. "You have spent the past four years in surgical training and know more than your mentors. You are a better surgeon than them because you have operated on every day of your training. Grow a pair of balls. You're going to ace these exams. And stop your extremely annoying habit of pacing." With that, she got up and slammed the door. She went to the spare bedroom and crawled into the spare bed.

That seemed to cure Jeremy of his anxiety about the exams. He now had something else to think about. Iona's rage. He fell into a deep sleep. The next day, he aced his exams. Once again, Iona had pulled him through.

"Well, I am happy that was all it was. I'll try to remain anxiety-free for the rest of the trip. I wouldn't want you to throw me overboard in a rage, " Jeremy said, laughing.

"I have never smelled anxiety or depression when you are at sea," said Iona. "I know that is when you are the happiest, and I love being with you when you are like that."

Jeremy smiled at that. It was true. There was a sense of peace and contentment when he was on the wide-open ocean with no other boats for miles and miles. He had to rely on his wits. If a problem came up, he would need to solve it independently. There was tremendous satisfaction in being self-reliant. He relished the uncertainty of the weather. Weather forecasting was reasonably accurate for five days, but after that, anything could happen. For Jeremy, it was just another problem to solve.

His cellphone buzzed an email alert. He opened the email while Iona went below deck to fetch them another cup of coffee. A weather system moving in would cause strong northeast winds of 40 knots. That kind of wind was the limit of what Jeremy was willing to tolerate. He placed a call to his weather router, Casey.

"It looks like there's a nor'easter coming my way," said Jeremy.

"Let me pull your positioning up on my chart," said Casey. "You've got enough time to make it to Charleston or Norfolk before the storm hits. Hunker down there for four or five days until it passes. The good news for you is the area where I predicted no wind would disappear. You'll be able to sail on a beam reach. You'll have no difficulty squeaking by Cape Hatteras across the Gulf Stream. I'll let you know when the weather window opens to get you to New York City."

"Thanks for the expert advice," said Jeremy. "We'll talk soon."

Iona and Jeremy consulted their chart plotter and adjusted the course to Norfolk, Virginia. *Iona Too* pulled into Little Creek Marina in Norfolk 3 days later just as the winds picked up. They tied up the boat on their assigned dock. They had checked in through customs using the ROAM app while at sea, using their Starlink Internet service. The app responded, "Your stay has been approved."

Jeremy and Iona sat in a restaurant near the Marina eating East Coast crab when Iona's phone went off. "There's a problem with your mother," said Dr. Jack Wilson. "The mRNA vaccine we gave her has failed to elicit an adequate immune response. Although she has hyper functioning T cells, we suspect they are just too old to allow for good antibody production."

"What does all this mean?" asked Iona.

"We have several options," explained Jack. "One option is to do nothing. The problem with this option is that the disease-free five-year survival is only 16%. Another option is to develop another mRNA vaccine using her tissue. The problem with this approach is that we have not tried it before and feel it is too risky. When we tried this in animal studies, some died. She, too, might develop a similar graft versus host response, which could cause her death. Another option is to use some of your T cells, which are also hyper-functioning, and see if this elicits an immune response in your mom. I have used this successfully in a few other cases. The key thing is your T cells are hyper functioning, which means they should produce an adequate antibody response. Because of your similar genetics, we do not expect that she will not reject your T cells."

"It sounds like the best option is option number three. What do I need to do?" said Iona.

"You will need to come back to Toronto immediately. We need to work on your T cell extraction," said Jack. "You will need to donate approximately one liter of blood so that we can extract the necessary circulating T cells. We are lucky because we currently have the best facility in the world for developing mRNA vaccines from T cells."

"I'll be there tomorrow," said Iona.

Iona booked a flight that took her to New York City with a connection to Toronto. She left Jeremy and *Iona Too*, taking an Uber at 5 AM to catch the 7 AM New York flight. Jeremy was alone again, thinking about how he would get the boat back to Toronto without Iona.

Chapter 13

Bruce had never been so excited about his research. He had developed the mRNA vaccine for Isabel's pancreatic cancer. He could not explain why her T cells could not produce the antibodies against pancreatic cancer. In the lab setting, they produced the antibody but failed to do so in response to the mRNA vaccine when injected. There were several explanations. They gave all the patients some potent immunosuppression. She might have overreacted to the immunosuppression agents. Normally, the resident T cells were less sensitive to immunosuppression than circulating T cells were. These resident T cells would normally produce antibodies against the cancer. Another possibility was that her T cells could produce antibodies because of her age.

His excitement stemmed from Iona Young's astounding T cell function. He had never seen such an activity. Despite potent immune suppression in the lab, the T cells could still produce antibodies against Isabel's cancer. Bruce was certain that he had stumbled upon something groundbreaking here. Bruce knew administering Iona's T cells to Isabel would enable her to produce antibodies against the cancer. He had already informed the doctors looking after Isabel that he had samples of the T cells ready to be administered to Isabel. The T cells were ready to produce antibodies against the cancer, as he had exposed them to the mRNA vaccine. They would administer these T cells to Isabel within the next hour.

The best part for Bruce was the excitement on Li Ming's face later in the evening when he told her about the T cells he had extracted from Iona. He explained how he made antibodies to treat her mother's pancreatic cancer that functioned well in the lab. The daughter and mother were genetically similar enough that he was confident the mother's immune system would not reject the T cells.

"The best part," said Bruce, "is that no one else in the world has these sophisticated techniques to do these complex treatments."

"That's what I find so exciting about you," said Li Ming. "Your brilliant mind."

Bruce beamed a huge grin. Li Ming was the only one who thought so much of him. His research had progressed faster than he could have imagined. It was all because of Li Ming and her positive influence on him. He would soon be on his way to fame and fortune. The thought of waiting until his contract at the research lab expired brought him back to a sober reality.

"Tell me about the daughter. What's her name?" asked Li Ming.

"Iona Young," said Bruce. "She's……" Bruce stopped in mid-sentence when he saw the shocked look on Li Ming's face.

"Are you alright?" asked Bruce.

Li Ming went silent for a moment, deep in thought. "I know her," said Li Ming. "I went to China with her and her husband, Jeremy, a few years ago. After showing them around, I organized a medical conference where her husband lectured.

"Tell me more about her T cells. What makes them so special?"

"They can produce enormous quantities of antibodies. I have never seen such hyper functioning T cells. Usually, T cell function diminishes after birth. These function like neonatal T cells. I can only imagine how well they functioned when she was little. It's too bad that no one else except a genetically similar relative can benefit from her T cells," explained Bruce.

"Is it possible to mix an ovum from a woman like Iona with sperm from a male with hyper functioning T cells? Wouldn't this make an embryo with super T cells from the thymus?" asked Li Ming.

"Theoretically, yes," said Bruce. "The T cells would be naïve, so they would not make antibodies against a foreign host. We could code them to produce massive amounts of antibodies in a short time, destroying the cancer cells quickly.

"Practically, the answer is no. Authorities across the world forbid embryonic research. Anyone caught doing this in any civilized country would go to jail for a long time."

Li Ming thought about this for a minute. Her mind was reeling. Weighing the possibilities, she had the beginnings of a plan in her mind. She would visit the Chinese Embassy in the morning and make another phone call.

Chapter 14

Jeremy had removed the mast from ***Iona Too*** in Albany. He was heading to the first 30 locks, leading him through the Erie Canal to Lake Ontario. After Iona flew back to Toronto from Norfolk, he waited out the storm for four days in Little Creek Marina. He used the opportunity to do some work on the boat. The water maker had been malfunctioning, so he took it apart and tried to put it back together again. There was an annoying leak from the hatch in the bedroom, so he removed the hatch and sealed the leak. The email from Casey describing a good weather window to New York City arrived the morning he had left. It would take 36 hours to get to New York City. Marina rates were $500 per night, so he motored past NYC until he arrived at a marina on the Hudson River with affordable rates.

The weather was perfect. The warm spring sun made for a pleasant trip up the Hudson River. In Albany, he met up with a sailor named Ralph. Ralph was a sailor whom he befriended during his last trip through the lock system. He offered to assist him in getting to Oswego, New York, where they would put the mast back on the boat.

The trip through the lock system was uneventful. Jeremy navigated through the Erie Canal and dropped off Ralph in Oswego. He sailed solo back to Toronto and to his yacht club. Jeremy hoped he could begin a normal life. He had been away for the past year. Iona was keen to start her work as a psychotherapist. Her patients missed her, and she missed them. Exactly how Jeremy would spend his days was unclear to him. Having left the hospital on unfriendly terms, he did not wish to go back there. He needed to decide whether he wanted to work in a private clinic. There was no rush to make any work-related decisions.

The CSIS visit one week after returning made him feel uncomfortable. There must be more to the story that the agents from CSIS were not telling him. Medical research was a huge money-making multinational machine. Having the ability to increase longevity by curing cancer would create huge profits. Canada had a great reputation for accuracy and honesty in their research because of intense scrutiny. However, the cost of human research was enormous. At some point, this cost would need to be recouped. Greedy corporations could profit by skipping research costs and getting cancer treatments for free.

Jeremy was sitting in the kitchen at his house in Toronto. It was a beautiful spring morning. He had just come back from a 10-kilometer run around the neighborhood. He was drinking coffee. Iona must have stepped out but likely would be back shortly because she had patients coming to the house office. His phone rang. It was from his lawyer, Michael.

"Jeremy, I think we have a problem. Turn on your TV to Channel 7 news," said Michael.

It was a breakfast channel station. The news reporter was a woman. She was a blonde, attractive woman in her late 20s staring into the camera. She was sitting on a comfortable sofa chair with a Channel 7 News coffee cup on the table with her legs crossed.

"We are here today to meet with a recent immigrant with a tough story to recount. She has been subject to things we did not think were possible in a civilized world such as where we live," said Sabrina, the host of the Breakfast TV program. "Why don't we begin? I'd like to introduce you to Li Ming Chang."

Li Ming was sitting opposite Sabrina. Her eyes were darting from the camera to Sabrina and back again. The right leg seemed to bounce rhythmically in a nervous tic. Her hands tried to find a comfortable position, moving from the sofa armrest to her lap. She seemed clearly out of her comfort zone. A million viewers viewed the Breakfast News Channel every morning.

"Why don't you tell us what has happened to you?" said Sabrina.

Li Ming cleared her throat. "I am about to be deported back to China." Tears formed in Li Ming's eyes and ran down her face. Sabrina reached across the coffee table and passed her a tissue. Li

Ming gently dabbed at the tears while she got herself together. "Let me start at the beginning. A few years ago, I fell in love with a Canadian man. He promised me a new life in Canada. He rented an apartment for me. I got a job, and I was happy for the first time. I became pregnant. Because he was married and didn't want his wife to find out, he made me get an abortion. He threatened to report me to immigration and have me deported if I didn't agree. Now, he is no longer interested in me. He reported me to the immigration officials. He said I lied when I filled out my application. I am getting deported."

"What a terrible story," said Sabrina. "Let me get this straight. You were a sex slave for this animal, and after three years, he is getting you deported back to China? The civilized world has outlawed that kind of human trafficking. Have you seen a lawyer?"

"Yes, I have," said Li Ming. "She is confident we have a strong case to fight deportation. My lawyer encouraged me to tell my story because many other women are in the same position as me. She explained to me that the only way to stop this human trafficking is to bring the story out in the open. Women like me must seek criminal charges against those men that engage in these kinds of illegal activities."

"Who is this man?" asked Sabrina.

"His name is Dr. Jeremy Young," said Li Ming.

Chapter 15

Jeremy choked on his coffee. He barely knew the woman, yet she was claiming on national TV that he had been sexually involved with her. He needed to talk with Iona. Calling Iona on her cellphone, the call went directly to voicemail.

"Iona, something has come up on national TV," he said to the voicemail. "I need you to come home immediately."

Jeremy called Michael, his lawyer. "What the hell is going on?" he screamed. "I hardly know the woman, yet she is making these claims. How can any responsible news outlet allow an interview like this to proceed?"

"Calm down, Jeremy," said Michael in a soft voice. "I'll tell you what I know. Just before that program was to air, I got a call from Sabrina. She remembered I represented you when your troubles reached national news last year. Sabrina told me what Li Ming was alleging you did. She told me they had receipts from payments for the apartment's rent. They allegedly have receipts from a weekend you spent in Niagara-on-Lake at the Prince of Wales Hotel. She said that they had other evidence as well.

Jeremy was silent on the other end of the line. "Why is she doing this?" asked Jeremy. "Do you think she wants money?"

Michael replied, "Something has never felt right about that CSIS meeting where the agents discussed Li Ming with you. There must be more to the story. I tried to find information on the internet, but it is sketchy.

"There is another thing for which you need to be prepared. I suspect that they have filed a criminal report with the police. There is a possibility that you might get arrested. I am going to work on that eventuality. There is a vast movement across Canada for women to come forward and discuss their abuse by men. Most claims have a legitimate basis, but a few women jump on the movement with false claims. The courts recognize these false claims are weakening women's rights."

Jeremy listened intently. It was not the first time they falsely accused him of committing a criminal offense. Last year, they arrested him after a patient died following the surgery. Even though they dropped the charges, many people still doubted his innocence. The incident destroyed his surgical career when he left the hospital under a cloud of suspicion. The positive part about the incident was that he spent last year sailing in the Caribbean with Iona. He realized there was more to life and happiness than career and status. Jeremy spent many evenings sitting under the stars on the ocean in the comfort of his boat's cockpit, thinking about his life. The conclusion became obvious. If you live life as if each day was a gift, then the next day would be even better than the last one. How things can change so quickly.......

Jeremy snapped out of his reverie when Michael continued. "I will contact the CSIS agents using the number on the yellow sticky."

They finished their conversation by promising to keep in touch.

Jeremy placed another call to Iona, but it went directly to voicemail. He did not leave another message. Just as he hung up, the doorbell rang. There was a woman at the door. The well-dressed woman was in her mid-40s. She appeared anxious. Her eyes darted from Jeremy to the room behind him as if looking for someone. "I have a nine o'clock appointment with Iona Young," she said.

"Come in," said Jeremy. "She stepped out for a minute, but I'm sure she'll return shortly."

Iona had never been late for a patient appointment before. After returning from the Caribbean, it took her two weeks to get her psychotherapy practice up and running. Iona was intent on providing punctual appointments. It was one of the key elements for her success in psychotherapy practice. For patients who had to wait, the anxiety would elevate to extreme heights, making it even more difficult to treat them. As a result, she was always on time. The patient who arrived for the 9 AM appointment was pacing the floor. She was muttering to herself something about the importance of punctuality.

"Where is she?" she screamed at Jeremy. "You said she would be here shortly. Well, shortly has come and gone. I'm out of here. Tell her not to re-book me. I'll find someone else." The lady stormed out of the house, slamming the door behind her.

Jeremy contacted Iona's assistant by phone. "Iona has not turned up for her first patient," said Jeremy. "I tried to call her, but it went to voicemail. I think that something has happened to her. Perhaps contact the rest of the patients for the day and cancel them."

Iona's assistant said, "This has never happened before. She is always on time. I'll try to call her every few hours, but I'll do as you suggest."

After another 15 minutes had passed. Jeremy placed another call to Michael.

"I think that something has happened to Iona," said Jeremy. "She has never been late for her patients in the past. Whenever I call her phone, it goes directly on the voicemail."

Michael answered, "Jeremy, something you have to be prepared for. Iona may have heard on the news about Li Ming's accusations. She could be having a difficult time digesting what she heard. She may want to avoid a meeting with you for now. I think it's too early to conclude that something has happened to her."

Jeremy said, "I don't think you understand, Michael. She would never keep her patients waiting. I can accept that she might be angry with me or not want to talk with me now, but she would not let that interfere with patient care."

"How about if we give this a few hours to see what happens before we push the panic button?" asked Michael.

Jeremy thought about this for a minute. He didn't have a lot of options available. The police did not accept a missing person report until they had been missing for 24 hours. Besides, he would not be on grand terms with the police at the moment, given this current set of allegations against him. He would need to make himself hard to find if the police came to the house to arrest him. He would try to make himself unavailable.

The conversation ended with the promise to reconnect in a few hours.

Chapter 16

The room was pitch black. It was stifling hot, and the humidity made the air thick. It wasn't easy to breathe. Iona did not know where she was or how she got there. Using her hands, she determined she was in a bed. She sat on the edge of the bed. There was a door with a tiny sliver of light coming through. She tried to stand up but felt faint, so she sat down again until the light-headed feeling passed. She stood up again and limped to the door. Someone had locked it. She had to urinate. As her eyes became accustomed to the darkness, there appeared to be a toilet in the room's corner. She sat down and urinated. After flushing, she washed her hands and face in the sink beside the toilet.

Iona made her way back to the door. She knocked at the door with her knuckles. "Hello, is anyone there?" she asked as loudly as possible.

Silence met her question. She made her way back to the bed and sat down. Iona remembered leaving the house at around 7:30 AM. Jeremy was out for a run. Her phone rang with an unknown number. She did not answer it. The call went to her voicemail. Iona dialed her voicemail.

It was from her neighbor, Lynn. Josh and Lynn had invited them to dinner last week. Jeremy and Iona were reluctant to go, preferring to get settled into their life on land. However, they were insistent, wanting to know about their adventures in the Caribbean. Jeremy and Iona relented. It was a pleasant evening, talking to normal people rather than sailors. Discussing things other than the weather and where to get parts for the sailboat's engine was interesting. The call surprised her because she recalled something about them visiting Iceland this week. Iona was mistaken.

"Iona," said the voice. "This is Lynn from down the street. Jeremy has been involved in a terrible accident. A car hit him. They called for an ambulance. He is at the corner of Shepherd and Watson. Drive there as fast as you can. He needs your help."

Iona tried calling Lynn, but it went to voicemail. She did not know what to say when the voicemail instructed her to leave a message, so she hung up. Iona remembered the sense of panic overwhelming her body. Her pulse was racing. She ran out of the house and into her car in the driveway. She remembered having tears as she went to start the car. It wouldn't start. She banged at the steering wheel with her hands and tried again to start the car. It wouldn't start. She was crying so hard that it was difficult to see through the windshield. She remembered the feeling of helplessness. Jeremy needed her. She was about to leave the car and run to the intersection when an oriental lady wearing sunglasses, who seemed somewhat familiar, knocked on her window.

"Can I help you?" she asked kindly.

"My husband has been involved in an accident. Can you drive me there? It is two blocks away," asked Iona.

"Come with me," the kind lady said. "Hop into the backseat."

The woman smiled and pointed to the backseat, motioning for Iona to enter. Iona hesitated momentarily, but the urgency outweighed her fear of getting into a car with strangers. She opened the car door and got in. There was a man in the front seat. There was another man in the back seat. Both appeared to be in their late 20's. Both were oriental. The woman was already sitting in the driver's seat. An icy chill ran down Iona's spine as the woman drove off in the opposite direction of where the accident was located.

Iona remembers a stabbing pain in her neck. Then blackness.

Iona lay wide-eyed on the bed. She tried to piece together how she got to this dark, stifling, hot room, but nothing else was coming to her. She heard the door unlock. The door opened, and light flooded into the room. A man with thick black hair and dark skin appeared. He was in his early 20s, about 6 feet tall, and was carrying a rifle strapped to his back. He was holding a tray of food and a water bottle. Without saying a word, he placed the tray on the floor and closed the door. Iona heard the click of the lock. Iona looked down at the tray. There were a few pieces of white bread and a bowl of what looked like vegetable soup. She was so hungry and thirsty that she devoured all the food and water. After eating, she tried to figure out what to do next.

Suddenly, Iona heard a noise outside the door. She heard muffled voices and the sound of keys jingling. Then she heard the door unlock. She quickly jumped off the bed and hid in a corner of the room, her heart pounding. The door swung open, and two men entered. They were both wearing balaclavas and carrying assault rifles. One of them grabbed Iona and dragged her out of the room. She screamed, but the man just tightened his grip.

They took her outside and shoved her into a waiting car. As the car drove away, Iona noticed a small logo on the door. It was the same logo she had seen on the car of the oriental lady who kidnapped her. She realized these men must have a connection with the woman who offered her help. Iona was terrified and did not know what was going to happen next.

The car drove a short distance through what appeared to be a small village. Iona noticed the palm trees and shanty houses that lined the road. The signs were in Spanish. They were somewhere in the Caribbean, thought Iona. Perhaps Puerto Rico? Maybe the Dominican Republic? It made no sense.

"Where are you taking me?" asked Iona.

Stony silence met the question. The two men in the car stared at the road before them. After 5 minutes of driving, they pulled up to a grey stone building. A silver garage door opened. The car drove inside an air-conditioned, clean room, stopped, and the driver turned off the engine. The armed men escorted Iona to an elevator. They went down two floors. They sat Iona on a wooden chair in front of a desk.

An attractive Asian woman walked into the room. This time, Iona recognized her. It was Li Ming.

Chapter 17

Jeremy was sitting on his boat. He had turned off the AIS Automatic Identification System to reduce the chance of anyone finding him. His boat radio sent a unique signal to all the other boats so they could identify him on their chart plotter. The purpose of AIS is to reduce the chance of collision. His chart plotter could see all the other boats that had AIS. He had anchored the sailboat on the other side of Toronto Island to hide. Jeremy covered the boat named ***Iona Too***. No one would know he was there. He was sitting with the same two CSIS agents who had first alerted him about Li Ming 3 weeks earlier. They had come by an unmarked inflatable dinghy in their usual secretive fashion.

"Thanks for contacting us," said Jeff. "You did the right thing."

"I had no one else," said Jeremy. "The police are looking for me so they can lay charges of sexual misconduct. They are going to have to find me first. My priority is to find Iona."

"Let me review what we know so far," said Ray. "You must keep this information private because if the press ever found out what we can do, they could destroy CSIS."

"We have satellites that continuously monitor the safety of Canadians," said Jeff. "They permit us to review the images only in extreme cases, like yours."

Jeff pulled out his phone and opened a video. "At 08:10 on the day she disappeared, Iona ran out of the house. She jumps into the car, but it doesn't start."

Jeremy stared at the video. The images were incredibly clear. He saw Iona bang her hands against the steering wheel through the windshield. He saw another car pull into the driveway. A woman got out and knocked on Iona's window. The woman was wearing sunglasses, but Jeremy was sure that it was Li Ming. She had a distinctive way of moving her hips as she walked. It was as though she was floating over the ground as she walked. Li Ming had spent a week with them in Shanghai a few years ago, showing them the sights. Jeremy and Iona had commented on her unique, seductive walking style. He saw Iona hop into the car and then sped away. "We tracked the car," said Ray. "It went to the Toronto Island Airport. There, a private jet flew them to the Caribbean. We tracked them to a small village on the north coast of the Dominican Republic. We think they are in a small fishing village called Las Tortugas."

"Why would Li Ming do this?" asked Jeremy.

"We don't know. We suspect it is somehow related to medical research. Li Ming has been involved with a researcher named Bruce. He is a world authority in mRNA research as a cure for cancer. You'll have to find out what Li Ming is doing and if Iona is there. You'll need to be careful. Li Ming is a dangerous woman."

Jeremy nodded. "I'll do whatever it takes to get Iona back, but why can't you send a swat team or something like that to get her back?"

"All we can do is gather information," said Ray. "We have no authority to arrest anyone or to venture into a sovereign nation and interfere. If we sent this information to the authorities in Canada or the Dominican Republic, it would raise more questions than answers. Questions such as how we got this information could prevent us from sharing it with you and others who might help. It would make it more difficult to get Iona to safety. We know for certain that you are being tracked using your cell phone. You need to get rid of it, or at least get rid of the SIM card and get another one. You need a new email and phone number, and do not access your bank accounts or anything else attached to your life electronically."

"I'll take the first flight to the Dominican Republic," said Jeremy.

"Not a good idea," said Jeff. Chinese-manufactured cameras are all over every airport worldwide. The Chinese have hooked them up to their Chinese telecommunication system. Facial recognition would spot you in less than 30 seconds. The safest plan is to take the boat. It will take you eight days to get there from New York City, but you must be careful."

Jeremy thought about this for a minute. He could get to New York in about seven days with his sailboat. It would take over two weeks to get to the Dominion Republic. The other option would be to put the boat on a truck and ship it to Annapolis. That would take two days. From there, he could sail to the Dominion Republic. It would take a lot less time.

"That's the plan then," said Jeremy. "I'll sail to the Dominican Republic and find Iona."

"Good luck," said Jeff. "Be careful."

"One more thing," said Ray. "We know Li Ming is lying about the sexual misconduct charges. We gave some of this information to the police. Techniques we prefer not to discuss were used to retrieve some information. We easily retrieved some of the information on the internet, which we gave to the police anonymously. You will immediately see that her story does not match our constructed timelines.

"Here is a package with information that exonerates you." Ray passed Jeremy a brown manila envelope. "The rice paper will deteriorate, and the information will disappear within 30 minutes after exposure to the nitrogen in the air, so read it quickly. Do not take any pictures of the material."

With that, the two CSIS agents hopped into their inflatable dinghy and returned to the city. Jeremy watched them as the boat became smaller and disappeared around Toronto Island. It was as if they had never been here, he thought.

Jeremy took the brown manila envelope into the main salon and sat at the table. He opened the package. The first set of papers were some pictures of the door of the hotel room in Shanghai. There was a picture of Jeremy and Iona entering the room with a timestamp of 21:06. There was a picture of the two of them leaving the room at 07:05 the next morning. A caption underneath said, *"No one entered or left the room between 21:06 and 07:05. The only person seen entering Li Ming's room was Li Ming. It was the night that Li Ming alleges Jeremy sexually assaulted her in her room."*

The next series of pictures was of a Google timeline. It was a timeline of Jeremy's movements, using his cellphone as a tracker. It showed him going to the hospital at 19:03 and coming straight home at 01:23 the next morning. There was no stop at the Prince of Wales Hotel, as alleged by Li Ming. Someone had carefully changed the hotel receipts to show Jeremy had registered. There were handwritten circles around the changes. There were pictures of

Jeremy in the operating room with time stamps of 20:46 and 22:09, proving he was there during the time Li Ming alleges the assault took place. Jeremy laughed. "They must have hacked into the hospital's security video system," he said out loud.

The final set of papers was the medical records of Li Ming. She was infertile. She had undergone a series of medical investigations. Medical investigations revealed that Li Ming had blocked fallopian tubes. They were so badly damaged that the gynecologist could not reconstruct them. There was no possibility of pregnancy unless she had in vitro fertilization. Li Ming couldn't get pregnant from sexual intercourse, as she alleges.

There were a few other satellite images of Jeremy's car on the highway and pictures from the hospital's parking garage, all time-stamped and dated. After 30 minutes, the images from the pages faded. By 45 minutes, all that remained of the pages was dust. Jeremy ascended the companionway to the cockpit and sat down. A slight breeze blew across the cockpit, picking up the dust from the paper and blowing it out on the lake. He did not know whether he should feel relieved that they pardoned him or violated that his movements were so closely tracked. His phone rang, distracting him from his thoughts.

"Hello," said the female voice. "This is Sophie, your wife's patient. I know where Iona is being held."

Chapter 18

Iona woke up in the darkness. It was hot. She recognized the room as the same one she was in before. She remembered Li Ming walking into the room and telling her not to talk. Iona asked her what was going on and asked why she was there. She remembers getting held down by two men while they inserted an intravenous into her left arm. Then she remembers trying to fight off her consciousness from slipping down a black hole. Now she was here.

The lock on the door opened, and light flooded into the room. A young man appeared, carrying a food tray and a water bottle. He was the same man that brought her food the last time. Iona sat up in bed. His eyes were darting around the room, and on two occasions, he glanced behind as if to check if anyone was there. He placed the tray on the floor and stood up. He stood up and turned around to leave.

"What's your name?" asked Iona in Spanish.

The man stopped in his tracks and turned to face Iona. "I shouldn't speak with you," he said. "Those are my instructions."

"You are anxious," said Iona. She caught the familiar pheromone scent of anxiety like a wet brown paper bag that arrived in waves to her nostrils. She fought the anger as it surged through her body like she had trained herself when dealing with anxious patients.

"Raphael," he said.

"Well, it is nice to have someone to talk with," said Iona. His head turned to look out the door to ensure no one was there. His eyes darted around the room before resting on Iona. The scent of anxiety-induced pheromones flooded Iona's olfactory senses. She struggled to keep her anger in check, so she kept silent.

"You know my sister in Toronto, Sophie," he said.

Iona's anger dissipated as she thought back to the trauma Sophie had lived through at the hands of sexual sadists in Toronto. Iona was still in touch with Sophie. She had completed a computer science degree at the local college and had a good job in the security division of a large bank. Sophie sent some of her money to help support her parents in the Dominican Republic. She had fondly talked of her brothers and sisters in the Dominican Republic. Raphael was the youngest of 7 children.

"You helped her," said Raphael. "She wants me to help you. If they find out I have talked with you, they will kill me. I don't know what to do."

"Why am I here?" asked Iona.

"Don't know," said Raphael. "A security firm hired me. My job is to guard you and bring you food. I brought you back in the ambulance from the research lab. A Chinese company owns it. I overheard them say that they are on the brink of curing cancer. You have something that they desperately want. Something about T cells?"

"That's ridiculous," said Iona. "Look, thanks for bringing me dinner and offering to help. I need to get out of here. Maybe you can think of a plan. You better go now before you draw suspicion."

Raphael turned around and shut the door. She heard the latch lock. She went to get the food tray. There was a slice of dried bread, some cold tomato soup, and a chicken breast. She was famished and devoured the cold food. Iona sat on the bed and thought about what Raphael said. She was in the Dominican Republic at a research facility. The rest made no sense. If someone wanted her T cells, she would happily donate them. They could have as many of them as they wanted. There was something else they wanted from her.

She lay down on the bed and closed her eyes. Exhaustion overtook her body, and she fell into a deep sleep.

Chapter 19

Huang Dong was staring at Li Ming. "You are an idiot!" he shouted. Li Ming was sitting in a chair at the desk. Huang Dong, who recruited Li Ming 5 years ago to her present position, towered over her in a rage. "How could you be so stupid?"

Li Ming stared back at Huang Dong. He was the idiot. He knew nothing about cancer research and relied on those in power above him for his information. Li Ming knew more about mRNA-based cancer research thanks to Bruce's information. They were onto something, and she would prove it to him.

"How in the world do you expect to get a viable ovum that we can use from a postmenopausal woman?" he asked, not expecting an answer. "I've consulted our top fertility expert in Shanghai, and he says that you are wasting everyone's time. It is just not possible. I want you to end this madness now and get rid of her so no one will ever find her and what you were up to."

"First, you need an education in mRNA cancer treatments before you call me names," said Li Ming. "Bruce is flying in this afternoon, and I advise you to spend a few hours getting up to speed with the research he has been conducting. He is further ahead than anyone else in the world. I have him under my thumb. He is infatuated with me and will do anything for me. You will find him a little odd. He is on the spectrum, but he is brilliant.

"Second, it is possible to develop an ovum in a postmenopausal woman. There is a process developed in Greece called PRP, Platelet Rich Plasma treatment. The treatment concentrates a patient's platelets. Initially, it was used to promote healing in musculoskeletal conditions. A group in Greece has injected the concentrate into the ovaries of postmenopausal women with excellent results. We gave Iona the first injection into both ovaries yesterday using ultrasound guidance. We will give her another injection tomorrow. I have scheduled her to have her ovaries removed in 3 days."

Huang Dong remained silent while he thought about this. He had set up this lab in the Dominican Republic because they could conduct any research they wanted without scrutiny or oversight. Many people of oriental origin lived in the Dominican Republic so that they could blend in easily. Embryonic research was illegal across the world. It was the ideal location to conduct this type of research in secret.

"Third," continued Li Ming, "Iona has some of the highest functioning T cells ever seen. If we cannot extract an ovum, we will use every drop of her blood to get the most T cells ever. Bruce thinks he can develop mRNA vaccines using an unfamiliar process but has not yet tested it."

"I want the ovum," said Huang Dong. "This is the reason we developed this lab. We need to grow embryonic thymus containing naïve T cells that any human will not reject. This is the key to a universal cure for cancers. I will say this once. Do not fail me, Li Ming. You know what the consequences will be."

Li Ming stared at Huang Dong. He was under a great deal of pressure to produce results. She had no doubts that he would carry out his threat against her. Li Ming had confidence that Bruce would help soften his stance once they talked. Bruce agreed to come to the Dominican Republic on holiday with Li Ming. She had booked them at a 5-star hotel, but she had also told him about this facility, and he was keen to visit the lab. Li Ming wanted to exploit Bruce's dream of having his lab and making a fortune from his research.

"Give me a week, and I will give you a progress report that will jettison your career to the top," said Li Ming. "We will have the results that you need."

Chapter 20

Iona awoke from her sleep when she heard the door unlock. It was the middle of the night. No light came into the room when the door opened. The pheromone scent of a wet brown paper bag drifted across the olfactory turbinates in her nose. She knew it was Raphael. He was extremely anxious. It also made her angry. "What the fuck are you doing here at this hour? If cameras focus on this room, they will send someone to investigate. Are you crazy?" she shouted at him.

"Shhh," he pleaded, "I don't want anyone to hear us."

Iona could tell he was slipping deeper into his anxiety. She would have to control her anger. "Okay, I'm sorry. You startled me," she said.

"I'm going to get you out of here," said Raphael. "The guard is fast asleep. I brought him a beer that was laced with clonazepam and waited until he passed out. There is no one watching any cameras at this hour of night."

"Where are you taking me?" asked Iona.

"I know every secret place on the island," he answered. "I will hide you so no one will find you."

Iona was not entirely sure that she could trust him. She believed he was Sophie's brother because Sophie had talked about him. Iona would need to determine whether he was telling her the truth. "How do I know you will help me and not harm me?" she asked.

"Look, we don't have much time," he answered. "You'll have to trust me. Sophie told me your husband is coming here, but it will take another seven days. I found out that they want to use you somehow to make a cancer vaccine that will cure everyone. Something about unique cells that are genetically passed on from one generation to another. I don't understand the details, but after they have finished with you, they will kill you. I can't let that happen. Sophie still needs you. You meet with her once a month and without your guidance….well, I don't know what will happen to her."

It was true. Even during the past year sailing in the Caribbean, Iona would do a video session with Sophie once a month. She could not abandon two other patients either; she would also meet with them on Zoom. "Let's go," said Iona.

Raphael had brought a flashlight. They crept out of the room and slowly passed the guard. Raphael shone the light on him. He was sitting on a wooden chair, holding his rifle. His head was against the wall, and he was snoring loudly. Every few seconds, he would stop breathing. It lasted 30 seconds, and then the snoring would start again. He was obese, with a large potbelly. He had thick jowls that shook with the snores. Undoubtably, he has sleep apnea, thought Iona. They snuck by him, barely making a sound. He suddenly stopped snoring. Iona and Raphael froze. Raphael turned off the flashlight.

It happened in less than a second. The guard bolted upright and flipped on the light. He was wide awake. He was in a rage. "You little shit! Where do you think you are going?" he shouted. The rifle was pointed inches away from Raphael's head. The pheromone scent of extreme anxiety wafting from Raphael saturated the olfactory turbinates in Iona's nose. She could not control the flood of anger that swept through her body. Iona calmly turned around and approached the guard. She stopped when she was standing less than a foot from him. The pupils of her eyes constricted and bore into the guard. "Stop, or I'll put a bullet into his brain," he shouted at her.

"You'll do no such thing," Iona said. In less than a second, she shoved her knee into his groin with such force it lifted him off the ground. He grunted at the same time he dropped his rifle. As he was falling to the ground, unable to breathe because of the tremendous crushing pain in the groin, Iona grabbed his right wrist. The weight of his body twisted the arm with such force there was a loud crack as one bone in his arm snapped. Lying on the ground, he stared at his mangled arm. At first, his expression was one of disbelief. He then let out a blood-curdling scream.

Iona was panting as she looked at him on the ground, screaming in agony. She contemplated her next move. Iona felt a hand on her shoulder. "Let's get the hell out of here," shouted Raphael. He turned around and began running for the exit. Iona continued to stare at the damaged guard for the next 10 seconds, wondering if she should kick him in the groin again before she left. She decided she had inflicted enough damage, so she turned around and ran after Raphael. Briefly, she lost sight of him as he went around a corner.

Turning the corner, Iona stopped dead in her tracks. An oriental man held Raphael in a headlock. He was holding a knife against his neck. Standing beside him was Li Ming. "If you want Raphael to live, sit on the ground now!" Huang Dong shouted at her.

Iona stood and stared at them. She could tell that the man holding Raphael was professional. There was a calmness in his eyes. She could detect no anxiety in his demeanor. His eyes focused directly on Iona's and did not waver. Li Ming looked nervous. Her eyes were darting back and forth from Iona to Raphael. The mouth was partly open, and she was hyperventilating. Her hands moved back and forth like she did not know where to place them.

Raphael was moving, trying to wriggle out of the headlock. The oriental man increased the pressure as Raphael's face turned bright red. Raphael's eyes looked like they would pop out of his head. The legs were kicking back and forth, trying to reach the ground. Raphael could no longer breathe.

Iona sat down on the ground. She watched what happened next as if it had occurred in slow motion. The man relaxed the grip of the headlock, and Raphael stopped struggling. He took a huge, deep breath. Raphael could now stand on both his feet. His dilated pupils, however, betrayed fear of what might happen next. In less than a second, the man's left hand, holding the knife, swept across Raphael's neck. He decapitated him as the knife severed the major structures. Blood spewed from the carotid arteries and arced across the floor, splashing to the ground a few feet from Iona. Raphael's body slumped to the ground, no longer moving.

Iona let out a scream. "No!" she cried. "No, No!" she sobbed uncontrollably. Within seconds, other guards appeared and forcibly lifted Iona and carried her back to her cell. She was in shock and did not resist. They dumped her on the floor of her cell in total darkness. She did not move from there as she cried. The tears were streaming down her face and dripping onto the floor. She must have drifted into a disturbed sleep. The sound of the door unlocking awoke her. She opened her swollen eyes as the door swung open.

It was light out when they came for her now, and they loaded her into a waiting car. Iona did not struggle. She followed them as if in a trance and sat in the back seat.

Chapter 21

Jeremy felt the warm wind sweep the hair off his forehead. The bright morning sunshine indicated that there would be fine sailing weather for the next few days. He was 200 miles off the eastern seaboard heading southeast, sitting in the cockpit of his 51-foot sailboat, ***Iona Too***. Jeremy checked the chart plotter. They were on course for the Dominican Republic. The chart plotter estimated they would be there in 6 days if they maintained the speed of 9 knots. It was hurricane season in the Atlantic. Jeremy had his weather plotter targeting three tropical waves that had developed off the coast of Africa and were heading his way. He would have to dodge them, but he would worry about that if that time ever arrived. He was going to rescue Iona, and nothing would stop him.

After the meeting with the Canadian spies three days ago, Jeremy determined that the safest way to get to the Caribbean and Iona was to sail there. There were cameras hidden in every airport in the world that would almost instantly alert the Chinese that he was on the move. Facial recognition technology would find him within seconds. These cameras are hidden in the security systems of every restaurant, bar and store in the malls of every airport. All the security systems were Chinese-made. The programmers designed them to feed the images into a massive database that tracks everyone passing by. Anyone with access to the database could easily track the movements of someone who flew.

Jeremy sailed across Lake Ontario for 60 nautical miles to Rochester, New York. They loaded *Iona Too* onto a truck and shipped it to Norfolk, Virginia. It arrived at 5 PM. Jeremy rode in the truck's cab. They launched the boat the following morning. After setting the mast, they rigged the boat. Jeremy was ready to set sail by mid-afternoon. It was a beautiful, sunny afternoon as Jeremy headed out to sea, leaving the sunbathers on Virginia Beach in his wake. As the boat was heading out of the harbor, Jeremy turned to his sole crew member and asked. "This is your last chance. Are you sure you want to make this hazardous journey with me?"

"Yes," said Sophie. "You will need help when you get to the Dominican Republic. You do not speak Spanish. You do not know where to go. I have family and contacts that will help us. I would do anything for your wife. She saved my life."

"We are in the middle of hurricane season. None are coming at the moment, but there are some tropical waves that I am tracking. It might get a little rough out there," said Jeremy.

"My whole life has been 'a little rough'," said Sophie. "The only smooth sailing I've had has been since I met Iona. Dealing with an angry ocean doesn't scare me."

Jeremy thought about this. He was very much against Sophie coming with him. He would have to make tough decisions at sea that could cause a bad outcome, such as dismasting or capsizing, to get to Iona at this time of year. The weather was reasonably accurate for 3 or 4 days, but it was anyone's guess afterward. He thought we might get lucky, but then again, we might run into a hurricane. Insurance would not cover a passage in the Caribbean during hurricane season because the weather was too unpredictable.

Sophie was insistent. Jeremy realized he was on the losing end of the argument when he discovered Sophie. Halfway to Rochester, he found her sleeping in the sail locker. At first, he was furious. "This is too dangerous a trip for you. I am going to send you back to Toronto from Rochester. How did you know when or if I would leave by boat?" he asked.

"I didn't," answered Sophie. "I've been hiding on the boat since you told me you would rescue Iona. You cannot stop me once I have decided on something. You only need to ask Iona about that. I'm coming with you. I told you that from the beginning."

Jeremy sighed. He had been living with a strong-willed woman all his married life. Now, he had to contend with one of her proteges. On the positive side, having another crew to share the night shifts was always helpful. It was a good policy to always have someone on deck to look out for other boats. Jeremy had turned off his AIS (Automatic Identification System). He would have been too easy to track if he had left it on. The AIS tracking is available to anyone on the internet. It meant he would need to rely on his navigation lights and radar for other boats to detect him at night.

The other benefit of having Sophie with him was that she was an amazing cook. Jeremy's usual practice was dragging a fishing line behind the sailboat as they sped south. After crossing the Gulf Stream two days ago, he tried his luck at fishing. He had been unsuccessful in catching fish until last evening. It was getting dark, and he would typically pull in the fishing lines at night and launch them again in the morning. That evening, the line was hard to pull in, and he would feel a tug occasionally. When the line approached the boat, he realized a fish was on the other end. Having never caught a fish, he did not know what to do next.

"Sophie!" he shouted. "I caught a fish! What do we do next?"

Sophie came running up the companionway from the main salon. She grabbed the gaffing stick, reached over the stern of the boat, and expertly hooked the fish under its gills. She guided the thrashing fish into the boat's cockpit with two hands. "Quick, get some rum to pour in its gills. The alcohol sedates them."

Jeremy ran down to the main salon and opened the liquor cabinet. There were three bottles of rum. He reached for the closest one, a bottle of Mount Gay, and opened the cap. The thrashing fish made it difficult to aim the stream of rum into the gills, and most of the rum ended up on the cockpit floor. The fish was still thrashing around the cockpit when the last drop of rum hit the floor, missing the gills by a long margin. Jeremy held the empty bottle by the neck and hit the fish on the head with the other end until it stopped moving.

Sophie looked at Jeremy with astonishment. "You don't know anything about fishing, do you?"

Jeremy stared at the fish and then back at Sophie. He was breathless from trying to stop the fish from moving. "What kind of fish is it? Do you think we can eat it?" asked Jeremy hopefully. "I've never caught a fish before."

Sophie laughed. "I can tell. See, it's good that you brought me along after all! We'll have an amazing dinner of Mahi Mahi filets tonight and for at least three nights."

Sophie entered the boat's galley and returned with a cutting board and a filet knife. She expertly cleaned the fish and threw the entrails overboard. She carefully sliced thin filets. Some filets she put into plastic baggies for freezing. Some she placed into the frying pan in a marinating sauce she quickly made. She threw the head and skeleton into the ocean. They washed the deck with buckets of seawater to clean the blood and rum from the cockpit floor.

The dinner was one of the best Jeremy had ever tasted. The fish was tender. It had a spicy kick that one can only find in the Caribbean by someone who knew how to blend the perfect ingredients. There was rice and fresh green beans. "This is the best! You must be a 5-star chef," said Jeremy.

"Once we have Iona with us, I'll make this again. I know how to cook. I looked after my siblings while my parents were working," said Sophie softly.

Sophie's phone rang. She answered it and listened without saying a word. Tears started forming and dripped down her face. After about a minute, she hung up the phone. Sophie cried quietly, wiping the tears from her face with the napkin.

"What's the matter?" asked Jeremy.

"They killed Raphael," whispered Sophie. "He was helping Iona escape. My brother tried to talk him out of it, but he insisted on trying to help her. They slit his throat. His funeral is tomorrow. They threatened the rest of my family to keep quiet. They will kill anyone who says anything."

Chapter 22

Bruce was sitting on the veranda of his 5-star resort, looking over the brilliant blue ocean. The long black hair covering her naked back was all he could see of Li Ming as she breathed quietly in her sleep. She had met him at the airport the previous afternoon, and a taxi took them to this beautiful hotel in Sousa. They spent the afternoon in bed together and then ate dinner at the restaurant overlooking the bay. The entire sky turned bright red as the sun went down. Bruce had never experienced such brilliant colors in his sheltered life as a researcher. He never imagined that life could be so vibrant.

After the sunset, they were getting ready to go back to bed when Li Ming received a phone call. She answered the phone and was speaking Mandarin to the caller. She seemed agitated, and as the conversation progressed, she began pacing around the room. Her voice got louder. It was always difficult for Bruce to determine when she was speaking Mandarin, whether she was angry or if it was a normal conversation. She hung up the phone.

"Sorry, darling, I have to go to work for a few hours," said Li Ming. "I'll make it up to you tomorrow." She planted a kiss on his lips and then raced out the door. It must be something important, thought Bruce.

Li Ming didn't come back until the sun rose. She crawled into bed and then passed out within 30 seconds. Bruce was awake by this time and got up to enjoy the sunrise from the balcony. He was enjoying the peace of the early morning and the view of his lover as she lay sleeping peacefully. It would be an amazing week. In his entire 41 years, Bruce had never been on a holiday like this. Life had changed for the better so dramatically since he met Li Ming. He felt as though he was living in a dream.

Bruce opened his laptop. He logged into the Toronto lab where he worked and checked on the latest results. The T cell transfer from Iona to her mother, Isabel, was successful. There were vast quantities of antibodies against the abnormal pancreatic cancer proteins. The response was powerful. This dramatic response was not one he would have predicted. There was something special about Iona's T cells, and he was determined to find out what that was. His intuition told him he was onto something here. The cure for cancer was within his reach. With Li Ming helping him, he would be rich and famous.

Chapter 23

The surgeon looked through the binocular lens of the DaVinci Robot. The picture was perfect in 3D. His assistant, who waited at the operating table, successfully docked the camera and the operating ports. The surgeon operated from a console in the corner of the operating room. He skillfully controlled the robot's instruments while sitting on a padded chair. He identified the right ovary first and then the left ovary, then he divided the fallopian tubes near the ovary using a harmonic scalpel. The surgeon divided and cauterized the round ligament. Leaving the blood supplying the ovary to the last step, he divided the right ovarian artery and vein. Enough length allowed for the laboratory to cannulate and perfuse with perfluorocarbons emulsion. It would keep the ovary alive until they could extract a suitable ovum.

The assistant placed the ovary in a bag and removed it through one of the port sites. Immersing it in ice water, the team rushed it across the room to a different area of the laboratory to be prepared. The surgeon then repeated the same surgery for the left ovary. He extracted it similarly. Having completed the surgery, the assistant removed the robotic operating ports. He closed the small incisions with dissolving stitches. They completed the procedure in less than 15 minutes.

Iona woke up in complete darkness. It took her a few seconds to orientate herself. She was in her cell from where she had tried to escape. Her mouth was dry. She reached over to the floor for the water bottle. An intense pain shot through the umbilicus and her lower abdomen, causing her to cry out. She fell back onto the bed. The pain disappeared in a few seconds of laying still and became a dull ache. She gently touched the skin around the umbilicus, and it felt like there was a cut that someone had stitched. There were a few other stitched areas in the lower abdomen. She did not understand what had happened.

A vision of Raphael getting his throat slashed passed through her memory. The memory of the fountain of blood splashed on the floor close to where she was sitting came rushing back in graphic detail. She remembered getting carried back to the room and dumped on the floor. She must have cried herself to sleep because when the door opened, the sound of the creaking hinges woke her. The bright light from the outside temporarily blinded her. They led her to a waiting van and took her to the same place as last time. She put up a fight and hooked her right fist into the face of one man trying to tie her down. The last thing she remembers was an intravenous getting started in her right brachial vein at the elbow. The intense pain of the propofol burned as it made its way up her arm. Then blackness.

They must have performed surgery on her for a reason not apparent to Iona. She was confident that she was in the Dominican Republic because Raphael had explained this to her. He also mentioned something about her T cells. She could not put the events together meaningfully. If they had taken what they wanted from her, why was she still alive?

Iona slowly rolled over on her side and reached for the water bottle. She guzzled half of the bottle on the first drink. Her mouth still felt dry, so she finished the bottle. She slowly sat up in bed and swung her legs over the side. She felt lightheaded. Sitting there for 2 minutes, the light-headedness cleared. She slowly stood up and banged on the door. She shouted, "Is there anyone there?"

There was no answer. They had locked the door, which would not open when she tried to turn the handle. Iona made her way back to the bed and sat down. She lay down and closed her eyes. She drifted off to sleep.

Chapter 24

Jeremy adjusted the sails. The wind was coming from the northeast. He was sailing on a beam reach, the fastest point of sail for **Iona Too**. They were making good time with an average speed of 8.5 knots over the previous 24 hours. Jeremy found that he only had to show Sophie how to do things once, and she could manage independently. It was great to have an extra body on board to help sail the boat on the journey to the Dominican Republic. They had made good progress over the past 2 days. With luck, they should be there in 4 days.

Sophie, hunched over her laptop in the main salon, said to Jeremy, "In the banking security industry, we have the skills to hack into any system. Daily, I would review the flagged events of the potential digital thieves and track their whereabouts. Often, we would find them in foreign countries and turn off their computers remotely. Sometimes, we would install programs to limit their abilities to go after us again.

"In Canada, the criminals would get a visit from the digital crimes division of the RCMP. They have yet to prosecute anyone because getting digital proof is so hard. At least, they tell the criminals they are watching them, which might act as a deterrent to some. Mostly, the criminals just laugh at them because they know there is no way for them to get caught. At the bank, we are on our own to fend for ourselves. It is like the Wild West of the digital world. Although what we do is illegal, we know they will never catch us. The banks have more money than the criminals, so we stay one step ahead of them."

They were hacking into Iona's medical records to see who had accessed her confidential medical files. The hope was to trace the trail back to those that had kidnapped her. Sophie had hacked into Li Ming's computer earlier, but they had found little information about Iona. However, they knew where Li Ming was staying in the Dominican Republic from her emails to Air Canada and a hotel booking app, booking.com. Bruce, a researcher, was staying with her.

"Look here," said Sophie. "Bruce has been in Iona's files frequently. The latest was this morning. He did this from the Dominican Republic. That seems odd."

"That's understandable," replied Jeremy. "He is the one who extracted Iona's T cells. They used them to develop the vaccine against her mother's pancreatic cancer.

"Look here, though," Sophie pointed to a line of computer characters and symbols that meant nothing to Jeremy. "Someone else has been in her files."

Sophie banged away at the computer keyboard. After a few minutes, she said, "Someone called Huang Dong accessed her records externally. The laptop he was using was in China. Everything on his computer is in Mandarin, but I have translated this into English to read it. Ever heard of him? It will take me a few hours to review the files to see what he is up to."

Jeremy had installed Starlink on his sailboat the year before. This gave him unlimited internet access from anywhere on the ocean. They charged more once the boat was further than 10 miles offshore, but having internet access for a sailor was a necessary safety feature. There was no way to function without internet access in today's world. Groups involved with the United Nations are putting pressure to declare internet access a basic human right. It would join the list just like clean water and shelter. Having immediate access to weather updates would allow sailboats to navigate away from storms in the middle of the ocean.

Jeremy headed up the companionway to the cockpit to let Sophie work on the laptop to proceed without further distraction. He logged into his weather app. One of the tropical waves that he was following was becoming more organized. The app predicted a 30% chance of this developing into a tropical depression over the next few days. It was too early to predict the likely path, but there was little doubt that it was heading their way.

Jeremy placed a call to his weather router, Casey Perkins. He answered on the third ring. "Hi, Casey, this is Jeremy Young."

"Nice to hear from you up in Canada," said Casey.

"Eh…." Jeremy said, stumbling, "I'm 400 miles off the Carolina coast heading to the Dominican Republic."

There was a moment of silence on the other end of the line. "Are you crazy?" asked Casey. "This is supposed to be one of the worst hurricane seasons in years because of 'La Nina.' You recall that La Nina causes less atmospheric stability when cooler water is upwelling in the central Pacific. We expect this to cause a lot of hurricanes in the Atlantic."

"That is why I'm calling you," said Jeremy. "Can you get me there safely?"

"Yikes," exclaimed Casey. "Several tropical waves are developing. The one I am worried about is heading right for the Caribbean. The modeling has given this disturbance a 30% chance of developing into a tropical depression, but I would put this up much higher. I'm looking at the tracking predictions now. According to your current position, I have you 4 days out from the Dominican Republic. If you boot it, you might just scoot around in front of it. Call me tomorrow, and I'll give you an update."

After hanging up the phone, Jeremy logged into the weather app. The circular pattern of the tropical wave was getting organized into a tropical depression. The maximum sustained winds were 40 knots, and the system moved directly west at 10 knots. It was 900 nautical miles to the east. He quickly did some calculations. There was plenty of time for the depression to head north or south. Chances were that it would change directions, stall, or fizzle out, giving him time to get to a safe harbor. Jeremy breathed a sigh of relief.

"Jeremy, get down here," said Sophie. "I came across some websites that Huang Dong was visiting. They are on the dark web, so not everyone can access them."

Jeremy sat down next to Sophie. "These websites have a lot of different rooms, so it is difficult to piece together what he was looking at. Why would he access a site that writes about artificial embryonic techniques? My limited internet information reflects that anything like that is highly illegal. I'm going to have to report this site to the RCMP."

Jeremy thought about this for a minute. "Can you wait until we get Iona back?" he asked. "We wouldn't want to alert him we are onto something here."

Sophie was quiet. "I'll cover my tracks as best as possible, but eventually, someone who discovers this site could track me too. I agree with you. Getting Iona to safety is the priority. In the meantime, I'll return to his computer and find out what Huang Dong is up to."

Chapter 25

Jeremy's lawyer, Michael, sat in his home office at about 8 PM. He had just finished dinner with his wife, Eloise. Since the last of his three children had moved out of the house three years ago, they had slipped into a routine. Typically, after dinner, Eloise would clean up the kitchen and put a few dishes into the dishwasher while he would go to his home office. Eloise would then sit in front of the television to watch her shows for 2 hours before heading to bed. Their routines rarely altered. Michael was reviewing the material an anonymous source sent him tonight. It was in a brown manilla envelope with his name on it. There was no address and no other information. The strange part was that they delivered it to his home address. Michael opened the envelope. A handwritten note said, "You might find this information interesting, but DO NOT share it with anyone."

Michael turned to the next page. There was a hotel bill from the Prince of Wales Hotel in Niagara on the Lake. Someone had circled some areas on the bill, showing that they had altered the names and credit card information upon closer inspection. They used the same font to type them, but words and numbers were slightly tilted, indicating that someone had altered the bill. These were the dates that Li Ming said she spent the night there with Jeremy. There were pictures of Jeremy performing surgery that night and a picture of his car in the parking lot. The dates and time stamps on the pictures proved Jeremy was at the hospital. A gynecologist also wrote a letter explaining why Li Ming could never get pregnant. There was more information to review, but the doorbell rang. For Michael, this was odd because they got no visitors during the week to the house. He checked the video of the front door on his cellphone app. The two CSIS agents had been to his office a few weeks earlier.

Michael answered the door. "I hope you don't mind us coming to your house," said Ray. "We parked down the street so no one would see our car in your driveway. If you prefer, we could come back or go to a restaurant or elsewhere."

Michael said, "No, it's OK, you can come inside."

The two CSIS agents followed Michael into his office. Ray said, "This is our typical visit. We prefer to go to someone's home rather than to their workplace. We park away from the house in case there are curious neighbors. Everything that we say to each other is in confidence. We came to your office last time because you invited us. When we initiate a visit independently, we try to make it as confidential as possible."

"How can I help you?" asked Michael.

"We met with Jeremy before he left. He told us it was OK to talk to you. We think he is heading for trouble," said Jeff, the other CSIS agent.

"I haven't heard from Jeremy in over a week," said Michael. "He called me to say Iona was missing over a week ago. He didn't want to go to the police because they were looking to charge him with sexual misconduct related to the Li Ming interview. I tried to call him, but he disconnected his phone. I'm worried about him as well."

"We have solid proof that Li Ming is behind the abduction of Iona," said Ray. "We have satellite images of her taking Iona into her car and driving to the Island Airport. A private jet took them to the Dominican Republic. We believe that this has something to do with medical research."

"The information you sent me anonymously shows that Li Ming has lied about the relationship with Jeremy. Why would she do this?" asked Michael.

"She wanted Jeremy locked up in jail and unable to leave the country to search for Iona. The police take every complaint about sexual misconduct seriously. The police do not want to be accused of complicity or ignoring the rights of women," said Ray. "We sent the same information to the police. They are not taking her accusations seriously until they talk with her again. They could not find her because she was in the Dominican Republic. She did not expect us to have the technology to track or hack into her medical records. Please do not show any of the information to anyone. Some would judge us as too intrusive into the private lives of our citizens, but the purpose of all this technology is to protect Canadians. Also, you needed to have no doubts about Jeremy's innocence."

"Where is Jeremy right now?" asked Michael.

"He's on his way to the Dominican Republic on his sailboat. We asked him to turn off his phone so they could not track him. The Chinese have video cameras in every airport in the world, and by using facial recognition, they can track their movements. The only safe way to get there is by his sailboat. He should be there in about three days," said Jeff. "We have some information we want to share with him. We think we know where Iona is being held."

"That sounds crazy," said Michael. "Why would you put him in such grave danger? This is not the firestorm you should send a distraught husband into. I do not understand how you guys work. It isn't right. Surely, you could mobilize a team to extract her and bring her back to safety."

"Look," said Jeff. "They limit us to what we can do. We have no authority in foreign countries. Our methods of getting information could land the agency in a legal quagmire, so we deliberately keep a low profile. Jeremy would look for Iona even if we did not endorse the trip. We're trying to help him. Our role is to keep Canadians safe from foreign intervention. We failed to do that for Jeremy and Iona. I agree Jeremy is not a trained commando or undercover spy, but you understand our role is to gather information. This entire information-gathering venture on protecting proprietary medical information has spun out of control. We are in a damage control mode, and we think you can help us."

"How can I help?" asked Michael.

"We believe he is traveling with someone called Sophie from the Dominican Republic," said Jeff. "Here is her phone number and e-mail address." Jeff passed Michael a yellow sticky with the information written on it. "We have been tracking her on Google Timeline. They are three days away from the Dominican Republic."

"If you can track her, how do you know others, such as Li Ming, are not tracking her as well?" asked Michael.

"We are confident that Jeremy's whereabouts are still secret. He turned off his phone and removed the SIM card. He is not using his email and sailboat tracking equipment," said Jeff. "We noticed some activity using satellite images on Jeremy's sailboat before he left. We have pictures of someone climbing into the sail locker hours before Jeremy left. We backtracked the person to her home, and it was Sophie. She has a special connection to Iona."

"I know Sophie," said Michael. "Our firm was involved with a legal proceeding where Sophie was pressing charges against a couple that were sexually abusing her. The couple are in jail. The last I heard, Sophie had a good job in a bank."

"Here is the map of where Iona is being held," said Jeff. "Can you email this to Sophie? Here are some instructions on how to gain access to the compound in the Dominican Republic."

Michael looked at the papers that Jeff had given him. He wasn't sure how much he wanted to get involved with this subversive activity. It could play out badly in the press if there was a bad outcome and it was later determined that he was sending the information. However, these 2 Canadian spies were taking a chance, trusting him with this sensitive information. He would have to think this over carefully before getting involved.

"I need to think about this," said Michael.

"I hope you don't take too long," said Ray. "Jeremy is heading into trouble. He is going to need all the help he can get."

The two spies got up and left out the front door. Michael read the information they had left him. There were details about the building where Iona was being held, the entrances, and the exits. The information they left had details about the guards' positions and their shift changes. There were suggestions on how they could approach the compound to get in and out quickly. The next few sheets described a nearby building. They claimed to have evidence that it was a research lab. They believed the research involved illegal embryonic medical experiments, but they found no proof yet. The CSIS agents suggested that more information would be forthcoming as they collected it. There was a final note cautioning them about the dangers and to be careful.

Michael sent the information to Sophie's email.

Chapter 26

Sitting in the cockpit, Jeremy looked at his laptop's latest weather map. A gentle wind blew softly out of the east, and the sun still shone. Even though the sun would set in a few minutes, it was warm. The warmth of the tropics was deceptive of what appeared to be coming. The tropical depression was becoming more organized and was heading right for where they were going. They had named this storm Franklin, with sustained winds of 45 knots. The modeling had the storm intercepting them in 2 days. Jeremy called Casey Perkins. He picked up on the first ring.

"Casey," said Jeremy. "Things are not looking good for me making the Dominion Republic without avoiding the storm."

"This is no ordinary storm," said Casey. "The prediction is that it will be a category one hurricane within 24 hours with sustained winds of 65 knots. The waves are going to be 12 feet with the strong winds. The wind will veer south ahead of the storm, so I advise catching the south wind and heading as far east as possible to avoid the worst. You can make 200 miles easily and then head west after the storm passes."

"That's going to delay me by three days!" said Jeremy.

"At least you will be alive!" answered Chris. "The maximum winds will be on the east side, so you must get at least 200 miles from the storm's center."

"What if I head west?" asked Jeremy. "The sustained winds will be 45 knots on the storm's west side as opposed to 65 knots on the east."

"It is the waves that will cause the damage to your boat," said Casey. "Besides, you risk running aground on the Silver Banks. This dangerous reef is 85 miles north of the Dominican Republic. Neither you nor your boat will survive if you get stuck on those shoals when the hurricane hits you."

"What if the storm changes direction?" asked Jeremy.

"The modeling has the hurricane going through the center of the Dominican Republic," explained Casey. "If it changes direction, it will probably track to the west. The most likely scenario is that it will follow the current track directly at you."

"OK," said Jeremy. "That is good advice. I will think about everything you have said before I make my decision."

'Head east!" said Casey just before he hung up the phone.

Jeremy heaved a heavy sigh. His primary concern was for Iona. The longer he took to get to her, the bigger the danger of getting her to safety. However, he would not help if he was lying at the bottom of the ocean. Jeremy descended into the main salon, where Sophie was banging away on the laptop.

"There is a storm coming right at us," said Jeremy. Sophie continued to bang away at the keyboard, unperturbed. "It will probably become a category one hurricane within 24 hours." Sophie kept on with her task without missing a beat.

"Casey wants us to head 200 miles to the east to avoid the worst of it," said Jeremy. "This will delay us by three days."

Sophie looked up from the computer but continued to hit the keystrokes with her fingers. "Hurricanes are a way of life for us in the Caribbean. They are unpredictable, despite what your weather router will tell you. You can decide whether to follow his advice or follow your gut instinct. I will agree with whatever you decide. In the meantime, I'm finding some interesting information. You want me to update you?"

"What have you found?" asked Jeremy.

"Huang Dong has a salary paid to him by the Chinese military," said Sophie. "He seems to have an unlimited expense account. I have tracked his activity for the past five years." Sophie recounted the story she had pieced together about Li Ming's parents and their hold over her.

"There is mention of a research facility in the Dominican Republic that he has been involved with. A conglomerate of Chinese pharmaceutical companies has invested about $300 million. Their expectation appears to be finding a cure for cancer. I'm still trying to sort out what is happening, so I'll update you as I learn more."

Sophie's computer pinged, showing that she had an email. Jeremy watched her as she opened the email. Her eyes widened. She clicked on the attachment, and her eyes widened further. Her breathing became rapid. "Jeremy, this email is for you. It is from Michael. He says that there were some CSIS agents at his house. They gave him some information to pass on to you." I'll print it.

They both studied the information. "Do you know this area?" asked Jeremy, pointing to the map of the facility where Iona was being held.

"It is close to my parent's house," answered Sophie. "I know the area, but not the building. I'm sure some of my brothers will know the place."

"They are using your email to get information to me," said Jeremy. "How did they know you were with me?"

"I suspect the spies used satellite images focused on your boat," said Sophie. "They probably saw me hide in your sail locker. No secrets are safe these days. Look at me. I can hack into most computers without most knowing that I was even there. They can get information in ways you and I could not even imagine. I'm glad they are on our side."

Jeremy thought about that for a minute. The description of the place where they were likely holding Iona was in great detail. They had plenty of time to devise a plan to rescue her. The information about the cancer research made sense. Iona was told that she had unique T cells that were hyper functioning. That might explain why Bruce was in the Dominican Republic. The abduction made little sense. If someone wanted to research her T cells, all they needed to do was to ask her.

"Can you email Michael and let him know we received the information?" asked Jeremy.

Sitting behind the instrument panel that housed the chartplotter, he looked at the map. He looked at the shoals to the north of the Dominican Republic that Casey had warned him about. He looked at what lay to the east. There were miles and miles of open ocean. The wind was shifting to the southeast. Jeremy thought about what Casey had told him. He thought about what Sophie had said about the unpredictability of hurricane paths. His gut instinct was telling him to keep heading south. Casey was telling him to head east.

Jeremy made his decision. He turned the boat to the east and hoped for the best.

Chapter 27

There were ten medical researchers in the lab, along with 25 technicians. They had all flown in from China 6 months ago. All the medical researchers had a PhD related to embryonic research. Most were originally from Shanghai, but some were from research facilities in Wuhan and Beijing. They had all volunteered to come to the Dominican Republic because the pay was ten times what they could get. They were told they would be the world's first facility to produce a cancer cure. This was a dream job for a basic scientific researcher.

Mary Lee was the lead researcher for this project. She smiled every time she thought of how lucky she was. They have banned embryonic stem cell research throughout the world. Although an embryo will produce stem cells between day four and day 7, they destroy the embryo by extracting them. They believed these stem cells to have the potential to produce organs for transplant. Curing other previously considered incurable diseases was also in the realm of potential uses. The lab had taken the embryonic research a step further. The technology could now have an embryo grow for nine weeks. They could then extract T cells from the 9-week-old thymus. They centered the research on using these T cells to produce antibodies against proteins produced by cancer. The embryo would self-destruct without the ability to produce its antibodies.

Mary Lee knew that if the world knew what they were doing in this lab, they could all end up in jail. The National Chinese Research Authority approved this research. This approval had come from the highest level. They had a contingency plan to evacuate if someone discovered their secret. She had been told that there were explosives buried in the walls as part of the construction to blow up the plant should that be necessary. For her, it was all about pushing the limits of research.

Mary Lee was from Shanghai. At age 45, she was still single. She balanced thick glasses on her wide nose. At 5 feet tall, she was overweight and had a tummy hanging over her abdomen that she could not get rid of. She spent most of her free time reading journals and projects related to embryonic research. Working at a research lab in Shanghai for five years, she knew more about embryonic research than anyone worldwide. When the opportunity came to expand the research into areas not yet explored, she jumped at it.

The testicle that was sent to her was an amazing technological success. It was alive and could produce millions of sperm per day. The ovaries they had alive by the same process were a different story. She had argued vehemently that they needed young ovaries from a fertile woman. These ovaries were from a postmenopausal woman. The incompetence resulting in this error astounded her. Huang Dong and his team had focused too much on finding someone with hyperfunctioning T cells. To assume that someone passed the T cell function genetically was an enormous leap of faith. There was no scientific proof this would happen. Yet this was what they gave her to work with.

Mary Lee sighed and shook her head—all this research and then to get fouled up with incompetence. The researcher in charge of extracting an ovum told her a few hours ago that it was not going well. She had found a few immature ova, but they were unsuitable. It was what they would expect in a postmenopausal ovary. She was still looking but was not hopeful.

Just then, Bruce walked into the lab with Li Ming.

"This place is amazing," said Bruce, looking around the room with glazed eyes. "You have every piece of technology in this one lab."

"Bruce," said Li Ming. "This is Mary Lee, the lead researcher." Bruce shook hands with Mary Lee.

"I've heard everything about you," said Mary Lee. "I've read your work on mRNA vaccines for cancer treatment. Has Li Ming spoken to you about joining our team?"

"I wanted to get a feel for this lab before committing," said Bruce. "I've never seen such a well-equipped lab. I am committed to my lab in Toronto for the next two years. They have me on a tight leash because I researched T cells and mRNA vaccines for cancer. All my good work will not benefit me because they have the right to the patents. Li Ming says that could change if I do a little work on the side for you."

Mary Lee took Bruce and Li Ming into a small conference room. She had a PowerPoint presentation ready. Mary Lee went through the research conducted to date.

"So, how do I fit into all this?" asked Bruce.

Mary Lee was silent momentarily, collecting her thoughts before speaking. "What we are doing here has the approval of China's top Research Regulatory body. We are going to find a cure for cancer. There are over 10 million cases of cancer per year. This results in a huge economic burden for our country. We could direct the money saved from cancer care to our military. We could sell the treatments to cancer patients in China. The government could direct this cash revenue to our military. It would make the strongest military force in the world. We want to be stronger than anyone else in the world.

"It's essential that you maintain strict confidentiality about what I am about to tell you. Our research is on embryos."

Bruce's jaw dropped. He was speechless. "That's crazy!" he cried out. "If I got involved in this, I could end up in international court and go to jail for a long time."

"Well, that's not going to happen," said Mary Lee. "We have an endorsement from the highest level of government to do this. There are contingency plans to get us out of here and back to China at the slightest hint of trouble. We need you to extract T cells from an embryonic thymus in about nine weeks. We will program these cells to produce antibodies against specific proteins produced by common cancers. The embryonic thymus produces T cells that will not recognize the recipient as foreign. It will incorporate the T cells into their immune system. The antibodies produced by cancer patients will cure them.

"If you agree to do this for us, we will pay you $1 million."

Bruce stared at Mary Lee with his jaw open. His current salary was $60,000 per year. $20,000 went for taxes. There was barely enough left to pay for his rent and food. He was getting used to living a better life since meeting Li Ming. Bruce would never see that kind of money slogging it out as a researcher in Toronto. He would disappear from Toronto. To hell with his contract. He could hide out, maybe even here.

"I need to think about this," said Bruce.

"There is a lot to think about," said Mary Lee. "Can I speak with Li Ming? You could wander around the facility. You can ask the staff anything and get a feel for the place."

Bruce rose and slowly headed for the door to continue his facility tour. His mind was reeling. This was the reason Li Ming brought him here. He felt conflicted. She was part of this cancer cure project. Was that the only reason she was with him, he thought? He quickly dismissed that thought. His intelligence fascinated her. They needed him to extract the T cells from the thymus. The embryos would self-destruct after that. This was like playing God. Creating life, then taking it away. If he didn't agree to help them, they would find someone else, and he would be out $1 million.

"You incompetent bitch!" yelled Mary Lee once Bruce was out of earshot. Li Ming sat down while Mary Lee tried to tower her diminutive 5-foot height over her. "What the hell are we going to do with ovaries depleted of ova? You bring her here, extract her ovaries and put us all at risk when there is no hope for success." Mary Lee banged her fists against the table.

"Look," said Li Ming. "She is just a few years menopausal. I'm sure that you will find some that you can use. You'll have to keep looking. It will just take one ovum. One extraction from the embryonic thymus will give you the most powerful T cells."

"What the hell do you know?" asked Mary Lee. "You have no background in science."

"I've been fucking the smartest man I've ever met for the past six months," answered Li Ming. "He knows more about these things than you do. He explains everything to me. This project will be a success. You need to stop interrogating me and get back to your job!" With that last retort, Li Ming got up, walked out of the room, and slammed the door.

Mary Lee sat in the chair in the conference room, fuming. She was so frustrated. She was breathing rapidly, trying to think about her next step. There was a knock on the door. The researcher responsible for finding an ovum walked into the room. "I found one!" she cried out. "I successfully fertilized the egg, and there is already one cell division. It worked!"

Chapter 28

The winds were picking up. Jeremy had put the third reef into the mainsail. It reduced the sail area by 60%. The jib was also rolled up to half its size. ***Iona Too*** was barreling along at 9 knots. The wind had shifted to the south, so the boat was on the most favorable point of sail. They were heading due east, the direction his weather router had suggested. The wind speed was now 30 knots, with some gusts up to 37 knots. It would be dark soon. Jeremy did a quick survey of the rigging. He had placed jack lines running down either side of the boat, and he attached himself to them. That way, if a wave swept him overboard, it would keep him attached to the boat.

Jeremy made his way forward by crawling on his hands and knees. The waves were causing the bow to fly up into the air. As the bow came crashing down, the entire hull would vibrate, and the noise was deafening. A huge spray caused by waves crashing over the side of the boat completely soaked Jeremy. Jeremy checked to make sure the shackles were tight and the lines had no defects from the turbulence. The rigging holding up the mast was strong and intact. Everything seemed OK. Jeremy made his way back to the cockpit. Sophie had been watching him. She had tethered herself onto the cockpit jack lines.

"We are not getting out of the way of the hurricane fast enough. The winds are picking up!" shouted Jeremy above the noise of the screaming wind as it caused the rigging to whistle.

"Let's go inside for a minute," said Sophie. "There's something I want to show you."

The two of them unclipped themselves from the jack lines and carefully made their way into the main salon. It was quieter down there, but the slamming of the hull in the waves made it difficult to keep their balance. Sophie opened the laptop. She opened the NOAA hurricane website. She pointed at the path they predicted Franklin to take.

"They have changed their minds. The path of the hurricane is now heading west, not north. If we continue with this heading, the hurricane will hit us directly," said Sophie.

Jeremy studied the map. This information was only 20 minutes old, but it looked like Sophie was right. "We can try heading directly south. If we can make 100 miles in the next 12 hours, we will miss the worst of it," said Jeremy. "That is if it doesn't follow the same path as us. I think the safest thing is to take the sails down and head south, directly into the wind."

Jeremy placed a call to his weather router, Casey. He picked up on the first ring. "Jeremy, what are your coordinates?". Jeremy filled him in on his position, his boat speed, and the direction he was heading. He told him about the wind that was blowing at 35 knots from the south.

Casey was quiet. "Jeremy, Franklin is not traveling the path that was predicted. It is now heading right towards you. You have 2 options. You can head north, or you can head south. Heading south will mean you will have to head directly into the wind and waves. If you head north, that is the most likely direction Franklin will take if it changes directions again, and it might be worse for you."

"I was thinking of heading south. I agree Franklin will more likely turn north," said Jeremy.

"Good luck then," said Casey. "I think you are going to need it."

Jeremy put on his foul weather gear and headed up the companionway to the cockpit. The engine started on the first try. He increased the revs to 2500 rpm. Using the electric winch, he furled the jib. He turned off the auto helm and pointed the boat south into the wind and the waves. Immediately, the motion of the boat became erratic. The boat would slow as it ascended the enormous waves. When it reached the top of the wave, the front of the boat would slam down, making a loud bang before accelerating down the back of the wave. Reaching the bottom at full speed, the bow would temporarily get buried in the trough of the next one, and the boat would come to a screeching halt. Jeremy attempted to take down the mainsail. He released the halyard holding up the sail, but there were still about 10 feet of sail still yet to come down. He yelled to Sophie. "Can you come up here? I am going to need your help."

Sophie donned her foul weather gear and ascended the stairs to the cockpit. She made her way to the stern of the boat, where Jeremy was holding onto the wheel. "Can you take the wheel and keep the boat in the wind?" he asked. Sophie nodded and took hold of the wheel.

Jeremy clipped himself to the jackline on the starboard side of the boat and crawled his way to the mast, keeping his center of gravity low. He looped one arm around the mast as he climbed up the 3 steps on the side to reach the boom. Jeremy grabbed a handful of sail and pulled it down. He did this 3 times, and most of the sail was now in the sail bag that ran along the boom. The work was strenuous because of the erratic up-and-down movement of the boat.

Jeremy heard a scream coming from Sophie above the roar of the wind and ocean. She was pointing to the front of the boat. Jeremy, still perched on the 3rd step of the mast, turned around to see a wall of water about to crash into him. He held on to the mast with all his strength. It was as if everything had happened in slow motion. The wall of water hit him with such force it knocked the wind out of him when his chest slammed into the mast. As much as he tried, he could not hang on, and he felt himself get swept away by the wave. It buried him under the water. He could not tell what was up or down. After what seemed at least a minute, the wave receded. He found himself hanging over the starboard side, held on by his rope to the jack line. It suspended him about 2 feet above the water. He couldn't breathe because colliding into the mast with his chest still winded him.

"Jeremy, Jeremy!" screamed Sophie. Jeremy could not answer because he still could not take a breath. Suddenly, Sophie's head appeared over the side rail. "Don't worry, I'm going to get you on board," she said. "I engaged the auto helm to keep us on course." Jeremy looked up at Sophie with a panicked expression. There was no way she was strong enough to pull him back. He could not tell her to launch the man-overboard retrieval system that was in the port locker because he still could not breathe. Sophie reached down and touched his face. "Everything will be alright," she yelled to him above the roar of the wind.

Sophie climbed forward and unclipped the spinnaker halyard from where they attached it to the boat. She crawled back to where Jeremy was holding on by his rope, reached down and clipped the halyard to his life vest. Crawling back to the cockpit, put the spinnaker halyard onto the electric winch. Sophie watched as she winched Jeremy above the lifelines. Jeremy grabbed the top lifeline and flung himself over so he was now in mid-air over the deck of the boat. Sophie released the tension from the winch and lowered Jeremy onto the deck. Jeremy lay there, not moving. He could breathe now, but only with shallow breaths. Unclipped the spinnaker halyard that had saved his life and attached it to the lifeline. Slowly, he crawled back to the cockpit and rolled onto the cushions. Sophie sat down beside him.

"You saved my life," he said solemnly.

"I saved my own life," she said. "How long do you think I would survive out here in this wicked storm without you? There was no way I was going to let the ocean take you away!"

They made their way into the main salon while the boat continued the erratic motion. The slamming of the boat would cause the hull to vibrate at an alarming pace. Checking the weather, it was obvious the storm was coming right at them. They were heading towards the shifting south path of Franklin. It was as if Franklin had them in his sights and was stalking them.

Jeremy turned to Sophie and said, "I think that I'm going to 'lay ahull.' It means I will turn off the engine, lash the wheels so they don't move, and we will bounce along with the waves and the wind. The original plan of heading south is not working. It will be more comfortable for us. Besides, the winds have picked up to 45 knots, and I think the worst is yet to come."

It was relatively quiet in the main salon, out of the wind. "Not being a sailor, I'll trust your wisdom. I'll come up to the cockpit in case you fall overboard again," said Sophie, making light of the seriousness of the situation. The two of them went up to the cockpit and into the vortex.

After completing those tasks to lay ahull, the motion of the boat settled. It was dark now. They both went to their rooms to rest, knowing that things were going to get rougher.

Chapter 29

Iona woke up in the darkness. She went to the locked door. There was a tray with some dried bread, old cheese, and a bottle of water. She sat down in front of the door and drank the water. Her abdominal incisions were not causing her pain and seemed to heal as expected. She had pieced together that she had likely had her menopausal ovaries surgically removed but did not know why. The only reason would be to extract the ova. Raphael had explained they were interested in her T cells. How would he know about them? Iona concluded they needed her T cells for research based on information provided by the CSIS agents and what they told her about Li Ming. Extracting her ova could only mean that they were involved with illegal embryonic research.

Iona did not understand why someone had not killed her yet. She suspected they kept her alive because if the ova plan failed, they could still extract circulating T cells and perhaps use them. Someone must know that they have kidnapped her. Raphael likely spoke with Sophie. She would have spoken with Jeremy. It meant that Jeremy would be on his way to rescue her. Why has no one alerted the police? The best explanation was Li Ming and her gang had paid them to look the other way.

Iona ate the bread and the cheese. It made her feel nauseated. She needed to build up her strength if she wanted to get out alive.

She would need to consume calories to get strong. An escape plan is what she needed. After finishing the bottle of water, she walked around the room. There was a small sliver of light coming from under the door, just enough to see. In the center of the room, from the ceiling, was a light socket, but there was no light bulb. There must be a light switch. Close to the door, there was an area measuring about 4 inches by 6 inches that they had recently plastered. Using her elbow to break the plaster, she could see there was a junction box that they had used as a light switch. There were 2 wires with plastic wire connectors at the end of the two wires. She tugged at the wires. To her surprise, about 5 feet of wire came out. Her initial thought was to use it as a weapon, perhaps a ligature around a guard's neck. When the wire hit the floor, one of the plastic wire connectors fell off, and there was a spark. The wires were live!

Iona sat on the bed and developed a plan. The guards would open the door 3 times per day, mainly to give her food. Maybe she could electrocute at least one of them. When a second guard came to see what was going on, she could disable him. Iona had some hand-to-hand combat training from one of the best commando instructors last year. She was confident she could disarm anyone within arm's length and cause significant bodily harm.

She filled the empty food tray with water from the sink and placed it in front of the door. She planned to drop the live wire into the water when the guard reached down to pick it up. Iona went to her bed and rearranged the pillow and blanket to make it appear someone was sleeping. She knew it might take a few hours before the guards appeared again. To loosen her joints, she did some calisthenics to stretch and Pilates exercises. She also meditated. She would need a rational mind, free of anxiety, to be successful.

After 2 hours, she heard the familiar footsteps of the guards. The army boots had a distinctive clop sound as they hit the concrete floor. Iona hopped up from her meditation position in the center of the room and stood by the door. In one hand, she held the plastic-coated wire. The door opened. The guard glanced at the bed, which appeared to have someone sleeping. He glanced at the tray and reached down to pick it up. In doing so, some of the water splashed onto his clothing and hands. "Shit," he exclaimed.

Iona used the distraction to plunge the live wire into a metal tray holding the water. At first, nothing seemed to happen. The guard continued to hold the tray as sparks flew, and after 10 seconds, the tray shook violently, covering him completely with water. A putrid smell of burning flesh filled the air as burn marks appeared on the guard's clothing through the wet patches. The hands clenched the tray as the contracting muscles prevented its release. The electric shock surging through his body contorted his facial expression as the facial muscles contracted. Contacting muscles prevented him from crying out in pain. He fell to the ground. As he was falling, Iona grabbed the plastic coating of the wire and pulled the live end from the tray. She held it in her hand. When the body hit the ground, convulsions caused him to bounce violently on the concrete floor. He was unconscious, but his body was still convulsing.

Within 20 seconds, the second guard appeared. He leaned over the convulsing body on the ground, trying to understand what happened. His partner was all wet and smelled like he had been in a fire. The second guard was massively obese and had an enormous belly. When he bent over to help the first guard, the back of his pants slid down to the top of his buttocks, exposing a massive crack. Iona rammed the live wire into the crack and shoved it down as far as she could. With his hands on the wet clothing of the first guard, the electric current flowed through both of them. The second guard began convulsing as he fell on top of the first guard. The live wire dislodged from his crack as he fell. Iona grabbed the plastic coating in case there were others nearby. After about a minute and no one appeared, Iona peered around the door. There was no one. She dropped the wire, leaving it at the entrance to the room, and started walking away.

A thought flashed through Iona. She turned around and went back to the unconscious guards. She took both of their cellphones and their wallets and shoved them into her pockets. Iona started walking along the route that Raphael had taken her before that madman had decapitated him. She came to a door. Cautiously, she opened the door. It led into an alleyway. It was light out, and as the sun was directly overhead, it would be around midday. She did not have a plan. She would need to think of one on the fly.

Iona stepped into the alley to complete her escape.

Chapter 30

Jeremy woke up suddenly after getting thrown out of their bunk. The mattress had covered him. As he moved out from under the mattress, debris from storage bins that were supposed to be under his bunk fell to the side. There was just enough light from the red lights in the cabin to see. He stood up. Jeremy was standing on the ceiling of his room. That could only mean one thing. They were upside down. He opened the door leading to the main salon. It was pitch black except for the lights from the instrument panel. There was just enough light to see the streams of water coming from the cracks in the companionway door. "Why were they still upside down?" he thought. "These keelboats were supposed to be self-righting."

Suddenly, there was a jarring motion to the right, causing Jeremy to fly against the cushions in the main salon. There was a force keeping him pinned against the cushions. After about 20 seconds, the boat stopped moving. The bilge alarm started blaring, indicating it was pumping water from the bilge. Jeremy sat up. The boat had righted itself. He immediately went into Sophie's room. He could not open the door. Something on the other side was preventing Jeremy from opening it.

Jeremy opened the companionway and then the hatch that was next to it. Sophie was lying on the floor against the door, preventing it from opening. He grabbed the flashlight that was kept handy in a locker near the companionway. The light shone on Sophie. She was bleeding. Jeremy yelled her name and then jumped feet-first through the hatch. He landed inches from Sophie. He felt a pulse on her wrist. It was strong and regular. He quickly did a survey of her body with his light. The neck and head were in alignment. There was a small laceration on her scalp that was causing the bleeding. He put his finger in the laceration, and there was no skull fracture. He pressed on the wound to stop the bleeding. Sophie stirred. Within 20 seconds, she appeared to be fully awake.

"What happened?" she asked.

"I think we flipped upside down," answered Jeremy. "I think we are right side up now. Are you hurt anywhere?" Jeremy was still pressing on the scalp laceration.

"I have a slight headache," Sophie said. "Other than that, nothing seems to hurt. It must have thrown me out of my bed."

"Push on the scalp," said Jeremy as he grabbed her hand and directed it to the bleeding area. Sophie applied pressure. "Ouch," she cried.

"I'll have to put a few stitches in," said Jeremy. There was a loud bang on the hull.

"Oh shit, I think that was the mast banging into the hull." He shone the light on the bow and saw the two forestays.

After helping Sophie back on the bed with instructions to keep applying the pressure, Jeremy donned his foul weather gear and headed to the cockpit. Shining the light on where the mast was supposed to be revealed, it was no longer there. He shone the light on the bow and saw the 2 forestays. He traced the forestays into the water and saw the sails and mast floating beside the boat. Another loud bang vibrated through the hull as the end of the mast crashed into it. This mast would make a hole in the hull, and they would sink. Jeremy raced into the main salon and pulled out the wire cutters. He needed to cut the wire shrouds and stay holding the mast to the boat before it caused more damage.

Jeremy attached himself to the jack lines and went to the boat's port side. Cutting the 2 shrouds there was easy. He then made his way to the starboard side. He also divided these 2 shrouds easily, but cutting them resulted in a loud snap from the tension. Making his way to the stern, Jeremy cut the two backstays. He saw the mast drift forward, attached to the boat only by the forestays. Attached to the boat only by the forestays, Jeremy crawled forward. It was difficult because the wind blew 60 knots, and the spray pelted into his face. He couldn't see. The boat was bouncing higher and higher as he made his way forward. He was worried the waves could bounce him into the ocean, so he kept as low as he could on the deck.

When Jeremy reached the bow, he understood he had to act fast, or the waves would launch him into the raging sea. The wind blew the rain and spray harshly, feeling like sharp knives on his skin despite his thick weather clothing. Jeremy tied himself onto the starboard and port jack lines, thinking this gave him the best chance of staying on the boat. He reached across with the wire cutters and cut the first forestay. It cut smoothly and quickly.

The second forestay was halfway along the bowsprit. Jeremy inched forward, holding the wire cutters in one hand while using the other to pull himself forward enough to cut the last attachment to the mast. Just as he was in position to cut, a gigantic wave crashed over the bow, pushing him backward. The two jacklines prevented him from going overboard and kept him close to the bow. He inched himself forward and reached the forestay and applied pressure on the wire cutters to cut. This would require both hands. When Jeremy let go of his left hand holding him onto the deck, another enormous wave lifted the bow with such force that, coming down, he was airborne. The bow plunged into a wall of water. It was all Jeremy could do to hold on to the boat. After the wave had passed, he was no longer holding the wire cutters. The ocean had taken the wire cutters from him.

Jeremy carefully made his way back to the cockpit. He was exhausted. He was worried about the grave risk that the waves would launch the mast into the boat's hull. The wind was blowing 65 knots now from the south. He thought about this for a moment. The wind blew the boat, but now the mast acted like a sea anchor, holding the boat into the waves. This would keep the boat perpendicular to the waves, making it less likely to roll over again. After all, maybe losing the wire cutters was not bad. He had read about a heavy weather safety strategy using sea anchors to hold the boat steady in the wind, but he had never read about using a mast. Usually, sailors would use a large parachute as a sea anchor. He had one stowed away, but having the mast as a sea anchor was even better.

Jeremy crawled into the main salon. Sophie was still on the bed, but the bleeding had stopped. Jeremy appraised her about what had happened. The boat was bouncing around too much to stitch the scalp laceration, so Jeremy cleaned the wound with antiseptic and put on a dressing. He made some tea on the stove. Although they had been upside down, the electronics still worked. Sophie turned on the internet. Starlink was still broadcasting and receiving. They opened the NOAA hurricane tracking website. The wind settled to about 10 knots, but the seas were chaotic, causing the boat to bounce left and right. Having the mast that was dragging as a sea anchor made the motion manageable. To their surprise, the hurricane website showed the eye of the hurricane directly overhead of their current position. Jeremy thought, "Not too many sailors have passed through the eye of the hurricane and lived to tell the tale."

"So much for weather predictions," said Jeremy solemnly. "We've got to get through the other side of the hurricane. The winds should be a little lighter, but we can expect a rough ride; with any luck, our mast dragging in the water will keep us in the wind and safe."

"Maybe we should try to get some rest," said Sophie.

"I'm too wired up from all the excitement to sleep," said Jeremy. "You get some rest. I'll watch over things as we expect the eye of the hurricane to pass in half an hour. After that, we return to heavy winds for 10 hours."

Jeremy heard the winds whistling in the rigging. He must have drifted off for a few minutes. He checked the bilge. The pump had emptied all the seawater that came into the boat when they were upside down. The bilge was dry. There was no water coming into the boat. Jeremy sighed an enormous sigh of relief. Rescue during a hurricane would not be possible. They would be alone until they were through the worst of it.

The boat's motion was settling down as the hurricane moved further east. As the wind died, the seas became calm, although there were still enormous waves. The sun had finally come out. Jeremy went on the deck to assess the damage. It surprised him at how only minor damage occurred from the dismasting. The forestay still held onto the mast directly below the boat. He could see the mast through the clear water. An idea came to him. Jeremy went back to the main salon and retrieved his hack saw. Moving to the boat's bow was easy now that the wind had settled. He attached himself to the jack lines and began sawing the forestay free. It took less than 5 minutes. The forestay snapped when he was down to the last few strands of wire, and he watched the mast sink to the ocean's depths.

"Now, if only the engine will start," said Jeremy to himself. To his surprise, it started on the first try. He put the boat into gear and set the coordinates on the chart plotter for the Dominican Republic, 200 miles to the southwest. There was just enough fuel to make it to Samana.

When Jeremy entered the main salon, Sophie was making coffee. "Let me have a look at your scalp," he said. Sophie lay down on the cushions. Jeremy took off the bandages that he had wrapped around her head the night before. The laceration was about 2 inches long and went deep down to the skull. He cleaned the wound again and then froze the skin with xylocaine. He carefully sutured the scalp closed with 5 prolene sutures. "I'll take these out in a week," he said.

"Thank you, Jeremy," said Sophie. She was about to say something else when the cell phone rang.

After answering, her eyes widened, and her mouth opened in disbelief. "It's Iona!" she cried. She passed the phone to Jeremy.

Chapter 31

Iona was sitting in a wooden shack with a tin roof. The rain was pelting so hard on the roof; the sound was deafening. She was dry, sitting on the wooden floor. She knew they would look for her, so she hid in an old storage shed in a field, at least until the rain stopped. A plastic bag contained 2 liters of water, mangoes, cheese, and crackers. She drank half of the water and ate a mango. She thought back to her escape.

After escaping, she walked into the first store she saw. She bought sunglasses, a sunhat, a beige blouse, and matching pants. The wallet from the first guard had $102 US and 10,100 Dominican pesos. She paid for the clothing with 8200 pesos. She turned off the two cell phones so they could not track her. The town was called Las Tortugas. There was a central area with a bus station. She bought a ticket on the first bus out of there. The bus had enough seats for 12 people, but there were only 6 seats taken. Iona took the seat furthest to the back and kept her sunglasses and sun hat pulled low to hide her face. It was a 2-hour bus ride from there to Samana. It cost $6.00.

The bus stopped at a few small towns and quickly filled. No vacant seats remained, and 3 children sat on their mothers' laps to make room for the adults who entered the bus. The road was bumpy, and the trip was slow. The windows were open, providing ventilation on the hot and humid day. Iona was sweating, but she remained bundled up to conceal her identity. The breeze generated by the open windows cooled her sufficiently, so she was comfortable. Motorcycles screamed by, some with 3 people wedged into the small seats. No one on board the bus paid her any attention.

Arriving at Samana, she was the last one out of the bus. It was late afternoon, but the village square was bustling with activity. There was a fruit and vegetable farmer's market, so this is where she bought her mangos, cheese, and crackers. She walked down an alleyway that was deserted. There was no one around. It was here that she made the first phone call. She called Jeremy's number, but it went right to voicemail. She knew from conversations with Raphael that he had been in contact with Sophie. Iona had memorized her number because of the frequent calls over the past few years. They did some of the psychotherapy sessions over the phone when the internet could not be easily accessible for one of them. She dialed her number. Sophie answered on the 2nd ring.

"Hello, Sophie, it's Iona," she said.

"Oh my God!" Sophie cried. "I'm here with Jeremy! I'll pass the phone to him."

At first, there was silence from Jeremy. He was having trouble speaking. "Iona! Are you OK?" he finally blurted out.

"I'm fine," said Iona. She was never one to complain. She would typically minimize any discomfort or fears to Jeremy.

They quickly summarized what had happened. Iona talked about her escape, and Jeremy told her about the sailing trip.

"We are motoring along at 9 knots. Our chart plotter says we can reach the Bay of Samana in 28 hours. Can you make your way to Puerto Bahia Marina? I'll call Gavin, the dockmaster. He will take care of you until I get there," said Jeremy.

"Yes, Gavin is a good man. I trust him, too. I better end the call. This phone belonged to one guard I had disabled. They might track the signal. I love you. See you soon!" said Iona.

Iona walked back to the bus station next to the farmer's market. There was a bus heading to Santo Domingo, leaving in 5 minutes. She walked to the back of the bus and tucked the phone into the spare tire wheel well. She checked she had turned on the phone and that the battery would be active for at least 23 hours. If they tracked the signal, they would think she went to Santo Domingo, a city of 4 million. Making sure the phone would not dislodge from the wheel well of the bus, she walked away. She headed to a footpath along the coast that would take her to Puerto Bahia Marina.

As she made her way along the path, the rain started. She could see the thick clouds rolling in just as it got dark. She had often used this path, coming to town from the marina earlier in the year with Jeremy when it was too rough on the bay to motor with the dinghy. About halfway to the marina, the rain became heavy. A tin roof covered a wooden shed about 5 feet high. A latch kept the wooden door closed to prevent animals from entering. Iona opened the door and crawled into the empty shed, out of the rain. The sound of the rain was deafening. Iona hugged her knees. She felt safe for the first time in many weeks. Talking with Jeremy earlier gave her strength. She closed her eyes, thinking about how great it would be when they were together again. She fell into a deep, restful sleep.

When Iona awoke, the sun shone through the wooden door's cracks. The rain had stopped during the night. The silence when the rain stopped pelting on the tin roof caused her to wake up, but she drifted back to sleep quickly in the pitch blackness. She calculated she slept for 12 hours. She drank water and ate another mango before crawling out of the woodshed. It was warm but not yet too humid. It was about an hour's walk to the marina, so she headed down the familiar path.

The Puerto Bahia Marina is an entry point to the Dominican Republic for cruisers. She would have to avoid the customs and immigration staff. She did not trust the police, as they might hold her until her captors caught up to her. The developers attached a hotel to the marina with an open front lobby that the immigration and customs staff rarely entered. She walked into the reception area and sat down in front of a woman with a name badge, Maria. Maria looked to be in her mid-twenties. She had the dark complexion and gorgeous thick black hair common with Dominican Republic women. The lobby was empty except for the 2 of them.

"Maria, could you call Gavin and ask him to meet me at the bar? He's expecting me," said Iona.

Maria smiled knowingly and said, "Of course." It wasn't the first time a beautiful woman had summoned Gavin to meet her at the bar. That it was 10 AM meant they could presumably have the entire day together before her husband returned from a fishing trip or some other similar adventure. Not only was Gavin a handsome man, but he was exceptional at keeping a woman entertained for hours. Maria watched as Iona made her way to the bar and sat on a tall bar stool. She heard her order a coffee. Maria called Gavin.

"Gavin," she said when he answered. "There's another beautiful woman here asking for you. When are you going to settle down with a nice Dominican woman?"

Gavin laughed, then said, "Keep dreaming, Maria. I'll be right there."

Gavin walked the short distance from the marina office to the hotel lobby. He was there in less than a minute. He looked around the lobby to discover no one else except Maria behind the desk at reception. Iona was sipping coffee and looking out on the boats tied up at the marina. She wore dark glasses and a sunhat, covering her head and partially hiding her face.

"Iona," said Gavin as he stood behind her. Iona stood up and hugged him. The tears began flowing as Gavin continued to speak. "It is great to see you, Iona. Jeremy filled me in with your terrifying capture and your courageous escape."

"I'm scared," whispered Iona. "I need somewhere to hide while Jeremy gets here."

"Don't you worry about anything? I'm going to take care of you until he gets here. He should be here in the next day or so. I've got a room booked under my name." Gavin passed the room card to Iona. "Follow me."

Gavin led Iona up the stairs to the second floor. They walked past the gym and along a corridor to room 210 halfway along the hallway. Using the card to open the electronic door, they enter a beautiful hotel suite. There were white marble tiles for flooring. A beautifully adorned king-sized bed with tasteful bedding occupied the middle of the room. There was a bouquet of roses sitting on the coffee table. A bottle of red wine and 2 wine glasses were beside the bottle.

"I'm going to leave you here," said Gavin. "You must be exhausted. Do not open the door for anyone except for me. You can call me through the hotel phone on my cellphone. The number is on my card that I left next to the phone. When I visit you, I'll first call you on the hotel phone so you know it is me."

"Thank you, Gavin," said Iona. "I am ready to pass out. I'm so tired."

Gavin left the room. Iona locked the door and placed the safety latch. She turned on the shower and washed herself for the first time in over a week. She drew the curtains. The room went dark. Crawling into bed, she fell asleep within seconds of placing her head on the pillow. She dreamed of being back on the sailboat in the Caribbean Sea with Jeremy. She was lying on cushions on the front deck of the sailboat, basking in the sun with the gentle waves rocking her to sleep.

Chapter 32

The water was smooth as glass as Jeremy motored the dismasted sailboat towards Puerto Bahia Marina. He was helming the boat by hand because it gave him something to do. He always thought more clearly when controlling the boat than when using the auto helm. Jeremy struggled to believe that 36 hours earlier, the sea was a mass of raging water trying to swallow him. He had been awake since cutting the forestay, which freed the boat from the mast. They would enter the Bay of Samana within the next 2 hours. From there, it would be another 3 hours before reaching the marina. Jeremy had received a call from Gavin on Sophie's phone that he had tucked Iona safely away in the hotel. Gavin was certain that no one knew she was there but was taking extra precautions.

The scorching sun beat down on the boat. Jeremy no longer had the protection of the bimini and the dodger because the storm had torn them off. He wore a sunhat to protect his head from the harsh rays. The breeze from the 9 knots of speed from the engine made for a pleasant warmth that encompassed his body as he thought about Iona. Her inner strength made her resilient, but would recent events crush her spirit? They had been through so much together, and all they wanted now was a peaceful life together. Jeremy thought about how, sometimes in life, you do not have control of events. However, as Iona had told him on more than one occasion, you had control over how you responded to events. So far, Iona and he had done well-facing dangers and getting through to the other side of them. Jeremy pondered whether this would be too much for them to get through when Sophie appeared with a steaming cup of coffee.

"I think you need some rocket fuel," said Sophie. "You have been up for 36 hours straight. Why don't you go down and nap for a few hours?"

Jeremy engaged the auto helm. He sat on the cockpit bench opposite Sophie. "Thanks for the coffee," said Jeremy. "I was thinking about resilience and getting through hard times. I wonder how Iona will fare through all of this?"

"When you say, 'all of this,' I can tell you it is not yet over," replied Sophie. "Iona is tougher than you for getting through hard times. I would be more worried about how you are going to manage after seeing your beautiful sailboat getting the shit knocked out of her. I am waiting for you to fall apart, but you have kept it together." Sophie laughed. "One thing that Iona impressed upon me was that as bad as things get, there is always some good. I learned from Iona to find joy in small moments, like a stranger's smile or a polite "thank you." After a while, bigger and more beautiful moments will take over your life if you let them. It just takes a slight change in perspective to head you in the right direction. Iona is the master at finding good in life. You needn't worry about her."

"You have amazing insight!" said Jeremy. "After everything you have been through and almost dying in a hurricane, you sparkle with positivity. How is that possible?"

"You can thank Iona for that," said Sophie.

"What did you mean when you said it was not yet over?" asked Jeremy. "I plan to scoop up Iona and head to Puerto Rico, where we will be safe. I can order a new mast and rigging, and we can sail off into the sunset."

"They killed my brother, Raphael. It sounds like they tortured Iona. I will not rest until I find out who is responsible," said Sophie. "One thing I know about Iona is that she, too, will not rest. Another thing, perhaps you do not know about us resilient women. I'm sure you are familiar with the saying 'Hell hath no fury as a woman scorn'? Well, you do not want to see fury in a woman after what they have done to us."

Jeremy smiled. He couldn't quite imagine Sophie in a state of fury, but he suspected she would be like Iona. The fury might boil inside her, but outside, she would appear calm and silent. Jeremy found it much easier to read men's emotions. When faced with anger, they had difficulty keeping their rage in check. Loud words, threats, and even physical violence, from finger-pointing to pushing, were all part of the package. As for women, understanding what they were thinking had always been challenging for him. He hoped Iona was up for the scoop-and-run plan, but his hopes were slipping away after the discussion with Sophie.

"Maybe I will catch a few hours' rest," sighed Jeremy. He headed down to his bunk. He fell asleep within a minute of lying down. The slowing of the engine woke him up. When he looked at his watch, he slept for 4 hours. He hopped from the bed and the companionway to the cockpit. Glancing around, he recognized the town of Samana and the bridge over to the island. They were almost at the marina.

"You made good time!" said Jeremy. "I'll call Gavin on the VHF." Jeremy grabbed the handheld radio and pressed the transmit function.

"Puerto Bahia Marina, Puerto Bahia Marina, Puerto Bahia Marina, this sailing vessel Iona Too."

"Iona Too, This Puerto Bahia Marina, Gavin speaking. Great to hear your voice. Come to your usual slip C67. We'll help you dock," responded the voice on the VHF.

Jeremy took over the helm. Sophie attached the fenders to lifelines to protect the hull from the concrete dock. Jeremy backed into the slip. He threw a line to Gavin, and Sophie threw another to one of the dock helpers. They secured the lines on the cleats to prevent the boat from moving. Gavin hopped on board. He embraced Jeremy. They both cried tears of happiness. It was a full minute of hugging and patting each other on the back before they could speak.

"Jeremy," said Gavin after they reigned in their emotions. "We have a problem."

Chapter 33

Huang Dong hung up the phone. He was expecting Jeremy Young, but not this soon. There had been silence from Jeremy Young for the past 10 days. Huang could not trace his cell phone. Jeremy was not using his email. There had been no alerts from facial recognition in the airports. There were only 9 ports of entry for sailboats in the Dominican Republic. After Iona's escape, Huang's men visited them all and paid the staff $200.00 to tell them if someone with Jeremy Young's description gained entry. Each staff member at the port of entry would receive an extra $1000.00 if they confirmed Jeremy Young's entry. It was not surprising that the customs and immigration in Samana had finished telling him that Jeremy Young had arrived at the Marina. He would reward them but caution them about remaining quiet about their arrangement.

Huang had called the Chinese conglomerate owners of the lab and filled them in on the progress. He told about Iona's escape and how that might make things difficult for them. He asked them to send more trained security agents to help. They dispatched ten highly trained assassins to arrive in a few hours. They had trained them to kill silently and then leave quietly, with no clues as to who was responsible.

Since Iona's escape, they had had no reports on her whereabouts. They tracked a call from one of the guard's phones to

Samana. However, the Google Timeline tracked the phone to Santo Domingo before it ran out of power and turned off. Despite searching, Huang's men found no one at the bus station in Santo Domingo who could identify Iona from the pictures.

With Jeremy's arrival in Puerto Bahia Marina, he expected Iona would turn up there eventually. He would send a team of hitmen to silence them both before they caused any more damage. They needed the lab to remain functional for the next 8 weeks while the embryo got large enough to extract the hyper functioning T cells from the thymus. They did not want interference from Iona or Jeremy to jeopardize their careful planning until now. Although Huang was certain they had limited knowledge regarding the research, he knew that Jeremy and Iona would figure it out.

Bruce and Li Ming were sitting under an umbrella by their hotel pool. There were few tourists, but it was hurricane season and considered off-season. They were eating a dinner of freshly caught Mahi Mahi. Li Ming was drinking a glass of white wine. Bruce was drinking a Coke. The sun was low on the horizon and would set in the next ½ hour. They had the perfect view, sitting at the top of a hill. They positioned the outdoor pool and restaurant to allow the best sunset view.

"How do you like it here so far?" asked Li Ming.

"I have never experienced such luxury. I could get used to this," said Bruce.

"How do you feel about the proposal to keep you on staff at the lab?" asked Li Ming.

"I feel like I could stay here forever. I am still unsure what I would do to get my million-dollar fee. Doing embryonic research in a place with far less scientific scrutiny is cool. I am okay with getting involved if it doesn't land me in jail. My work until now has focused on getting T cells from tissue and then developing the mRNA vaccine. The production of antibodies against the proteins created by the cancer is my area of expertise."

"Let me fill you in," said Li Ming. "Imagine that you could work with embryonic T cells where there had been no exposure to antigens. You told me that the most powerful T cells are those that have not yet produced antibodies. The thymus of the embryo would be the best place to extract those cells. Now imagine if we had made the embryo from two individuals with a genetic predisposition to produce hyperfunctioning T cells. If we could extract the T cells and use them to make antibodies using mRNA technology, we could inject them into anyone. The recipient would not reject the T cells because they are so immature, but they would allow the host to make antibodies against their cancer."

"So," said Bruce. "My job would be to extract those T cells from the embryonic thymus so they could be used to cure cancer?"

"Imagine how powerful a country could be if they had a cure for cancer. Healthcare costs are weakening the economies of all superpowers. Imagine how much better off everyone will be," said Li Ming. "You'll be the hero in the story. The million dollars is only the beginning of your fortune."

Bruce thought about this for a minute. Before he could answer, Li Ming's phone went off.

"Hello," she said.

"I need to meet with you and Bruce," said Huang. "Can you come to my office now?"

"Give us ½ hour, we're finishing dinner," said Li Ming.

"Screw your dinner," said Huang angrily. "There is a car waiting for you just outside the lobby. Don't keep him waiting." The phone went dead.

"Asshole," said Li Ming in Mandarin to the dead phone.

Li Ming and Bruce arrived at the office, where Huang sat behind a large desk. He was banging away at the keyboard of his computer and barely looked up when they entered. Li Ming and

Bruce sat in the chairs before the desk and waited until Huang finished his task.

Looking up at them, Huang smiled at Bruce. "What is the chance of retrieving T cells from the embryo before 9 weeks?" he asked.

Bruce stared at him. "Don't know," he said. "I've never done this kind of research. My limited understanding is that the thymus gland is too immature until then, so it seems unlikely to be successful. I think it would be easier to retrieve them if we could wait until the embryo was 12-14 weeks. After extraction of the T cells, the embryo will die because it cannot fight off infection. So, the key would be to wait as long as possible."

"We've had a complication," said Huang. "The female donor of the ovum escaped. We may need to shut down the facility sooner than we were expecting. Don't worry about your involvement. We will still pay you a million dollars for extracting the T cells, and if successful, we could hire you full-time. Your salary will be 5 million a year with the possibility of stock options. We are planning on moving the plant to China. One plan involves freezing the embryo and restarting the process once we have moved. The issue with that plan is that it might take a few months to organize, as the laboratory is still under construction. I work for a company that wants results as soon as possible. They have not yet finished setting up the lab. We have tight timelines."

Bruce stood up. He walked out the door and slammed it shut. He was muttering to himself as he walked down the hallway and past the guards at the front entrance. Bruce exited onto the street and started walking back to the hotel. Huang and Li Ming stood at the window and watched him walk away.

"What the fuck was that about?" yelled Huang.

Li Ming stared at him, not saying anything for 30 seconds. She was seething inside. "Your asshole. You have no idea how to manage someone like Bruce. I admit he is a little odd, but I know him very well after having been with him for over 6 months. You do not talk to him like that. I am sure he is on the spectrum of autism. You do not discuss options. He wants to hear certainties. He can only focus on one thing at a time. Bruce is brilliant but socially inept. I will have to spend hours soothing his confused mind, thanks to you. He does not want to hear about the possibility of moving to China. Do not discuss escaped donors or ask him to get involved earlier than originally planned. He cannot understand quickly enough, and it makes him angry. If you want success, let me and I alone deal with discussions involving Bruce."

Huang glared at Li Ming. "Do not tell me what to do or say. You are the reason we are in this mess. I remind you that you are the one responsible for bringing Iona here. She has been nothing but trouble."

"You got your embryo," Li Ming shot back. "Don't blame me for your incompetence in hiring useless guards. I have done everything you have asked of me. You still need me if you want Bruce, the world's expert at extracting T cells from tissue. You had better change your attitude. I've had enough of your bullying."

Huang sat down behind his desk. Li Ming stood, staring at him with her hands on her hips. "You are right," he whispered. "I have been unreasonable with you. You have done everything I have asked of you. If you could sort things out with Bruce, I would be most appreciative. I have been under a lot of stress because of the escape. I should have killed her when I had the chance."

Li Ming continued to stare at him. That was as close to an apology as she was going to get. She knew she had the upper hand. Bruce would do anything for her. He was infatuated with her. She knew she could keep Huang in check by being the only one who could manipulate Bruce. She smiled at Huang. "No worries. It has been a difficult time for all of us. After the night I am about to give to Bruce, he'll do anything I ask."

Li Ming walked out of the office and into the street. The driver was waiting for her. He drove her back to the hotel. She walked past the lobby and took the elevator to her floor. She opened the door to the room. Bruce was waiting for her on the bed with his hands behind his head. He smiled at her. He was naked.

Chapter 34

Gavin was sitting in his office at the marina. He was thinking about Iona and how to keep her safe. There were cameras throughout the hotel. If someone could access them, they would see a woman going into the hallway of room 210. Iona covered her face by wearing dark glasses and a sunhat so they would not know it was her. Gavin knew that as soon as Jeremy arrived, the thugs would know Iona was nearby. It wouldn't take long for them to search the videos for a woman. Gavin chose room 210 because that was the room he usually used. The video cameras in the hallway would show the two walking down towards the room, but the image would cut out before they entered room 210. There was a small alcove which blocked the view. Knowing where the video cameras were located, Gavin would position his head so no one could identify him.

Gavin was 28 years old. He had been the manager of the marina for the past 5 years. Gavin knew he was attractive. He had the dark complexion of a Dominican and was physically fit. Working out in the gym 2 hours a day gave him a perfect abdominal six-pack. He spoke English with a Spanish accent in a deep voice. When he smiled, dimples would appear on the side of his mouth. When he walked, there was a slight bounce to his step that women unconsciously perceived as an untamed wildness. He presented the entire package as exotic masculinity, causing women to imagine what he would be like in bed.

They drew sailors to the marina because it provided great protection from storms in Samana Bay. They would arrive from around the globe to go whale watching and experience eco-tours that made the Dominican Republic famous. The marina was connected to a luxury hotel, providing visitors access to swimming pools, restaurants, bars, and more. Another major advantage was it was close to an international airport. Husbands often flew home for business, leaving their wives to tend to their sailboats. This was how Gavin became known throughout the sailing community.

The first time it happened was 5 years earlier. The marina sponsored a welcome party every few weeks for the sailors. Fiona, an attractive woman in her early 50s, was on her 3rd rum punch. She was sitting on a sofa in the outdoor foyer of the hotel by herself, looking at the party that surrounded her. About 20 other sailors were milling about, laughing, and telling sailing stories. Gavin walked by the sofa and said, "Fiona, you look lovely tonight."

"Ha Ha," she laughed. "The sexiest man on the planet says I look lovely. I haven't heard a compliment like that for years."

Gavin stopped walking and turned to her. "It's true. Just because guys don't tell you stuff doesn't mean they don't think it. They do not want to make your husband, Mark, jealous."

"No chance of that," said Fiona. "He flew to Chicago this morning and won't return for a week. I checked into the hotel. I need a break from the sailboat." She stood up and faced Gavin. She reached around the back of his tight blue jeans and stuffed an electronic room key into his back pocket. "I'm in room 210," she whispered.

The rest of the week was a blur. They spent the nights making love, and Gavin would get up blurry-eyed at 7 AM to begin work. Fiona would sleep for most of the day. She would wake up rested before coming to the restaurant for dinner and drinks at around 8 PM. They would repeat the sexual antics for the rest of the night. By the end of the week, Gavin was exhausted. He was glad to see Mark arrive by taxi from the window of his marina office late one afternoon.

Fiona dropped by the marina office the following morning. She was carrying 2 cups of coffee and offered one to Gavin. She sat on the chair in front of the desk where he was sitting. Fiona was crying.

"Mark wants to leave for Punta Cana first thing in the morning," she said through tears. "That was the best week of sex I have had in my life. I didn't know it was possible to feel like that at my age. I don't know how to thank you. I am so sad to be leaving you." She sobbed uncontrollably.

Gavin stared at her softly. She was a beautiful woman. It was sad that her husband didn't treat her like a goddess every day. She had a tenderness that Gavin had not experienced with a woman before. He was going to miss her, too.

She continued to weep. She opened her beach bag and gave an envelope to Gavin. Without another word, she left the office, drying her eyes. Gavin watched her walk away as she closed the office door behind her. He opened the envelope. Inside was $3000.00. A note with "Thank you" she had written in a blue pen. Written in red lipstick was another message: "Just ask for Gavin!"

That is how Gavin became known throughout the sailing community in the Caribbean. The message spread like wildfire. "Just ask for Gavin!" appeared repeatedly on the social media pages of Facebook and Instagram. The female sailors knew what it meant. Their male counterparts remained clueless as to the context of the message. The marina became even more popular as a stopover.

Chapter 35

Jeremy was sitting in the air-conditioned main salon of his boat. The customs officials were checking under the cushions and in all the lockers. They said they were looking for contraband, but Jeremy knew they were looking for clues to lead them to Iona. The two men were friendly enough. They both appeared to be in their 30s and were slim. They strapped the pistols to their hips. Their dark complexions were typical of the Dominican Republic. With limited English, they did not converse unless they had a question about opening a cabinet or another question regarding their search. Unable to find anything of significance, after ½ hour, they signed some papers and gave them to Jeremy. They left the boat and headed back to their office.

Jeremy went up to the cockpit and sat down with Sophie. "What are your plans now?" asked Jeremy.

"My first stop will be to see my parents, then my brothers and sisters," said Sophie. "I want to find out what happened to Raphael. My oldest brother is coming to pick me up. He's the only one in the family who has a car. He should be here in about 1 hour. I'll come back here tomorrow. Then we can look for Iona."

"Gavin explained to me she is safe," said Jeremy. "The research lab paid the customs officers to report if they saw me.

Gavin overheard them talking on the phone because his office was next to their office. They did not attempt to hide the fact that they were getting paid for information. Gavin told me the corruption here is rampant. They are watching us as we are speaking. Do not look now, but a man on the red speedboat is staring at us now using binoculars. He is on A dock, 2 rows down from us."

"I think they expect us to lead them to Iona," said Sophie. "I suspect they will follow me when I visit my family. My brother will lose them on some back roads. I already warned him, so he has a plan."

"I need to think how I can keep Iona safe, but I need to see her," said Jeremy. "Gavin is working on a plan. He says there is a shoot-to-kill order on her, and once they have killed her, they have a shoot-to-kill order on me. He worries they will access the hotel video and see the room where Iona is hiding. They know about you as well. They will come after you to get you to say where Iona is hiding."

Sophie sat quietly in the cockpit. She went into the main salon and came up with her computer. It took her about 15 minutes, but she could hack into the hotel's security system. She unlocked the videos and started scrolling through the files. Jeremy watched the videos with her. On the day that Iona arrived at the hotel, she saw her walk across the lobby to the receptionist. After a brief conversation, they saw Iona sit down at the bar. The server brought her a coffee. They saw someone who could be Gavin appear in the video. They did not see his face in the imaging. Walking together, they went in the elevator.

They looked at the second-floor video. Again, they never saw Gavin's face. Iona had dark glasses and a sun hat covering her face. An alcove blocked the view as they walked past.

Sophie deleted the segments of the video that had Iona. She extended the empty videos so it looked like no one was there. After clicking save, Sophie exited the security system and turned off her computer. She looked up at Jeremy and said with a satisfying smile, "It looks like Iona was never here."

Sophie answered her phone when it rang. "I'll be right there," she said.

When she hung up, she turned to Jeremy and said, "It's my brother. He's here to pick me up. Call me later."

Jeremy watched as Sophie hopped off the swim platform onto the dock. She waved to Jeremy as she walked through the outdoor lobby of the hotel to the parking lot, where her brother waited in a car. He went to the captain's table and retrieved his cell phone. He had turned it off for the past 2 weeks. The phone still had a full charge. Using WhatsApp, he placed a call to Gavin.

"Hi Gavin, can we meet? I'd like to see Iona." He said when Gavin answered.

"Come to the marina office. I have a plan," said Gavin.

Jeremy hopped off the boat and walked to the marina office. He closed the door behind him. Gavin was sitting at the desk. He put his fingers to his lips, indicating not to say a word. He gestured with his finger to follow him. Gavin opened a closet door. They walked in and closed the door. Gavin turned on the light. There was a false wall at the back of the closet. Gavin opened the false wall, which led into a hallway with dull lighting. They walked along the hallway until they came to some stairs. Gavin turned to Jeremy and said, "Here's the plan. We'll go to the second floor and enter the duct system, leading us to Iona's room. I had to use it once while entertaining a lady friend, and her husband returned a day earlier than expected. I escaped through the duct system in the bathroom unscathed."

Jeremy smiled. "Why are you doing all this for us, Gavin? If they find out you helped us, they will kill you, too."

"My life here in the Dominican Republic is a dead end," said Gavi softly. "I love the marina, but a time will come when I'll either be out of a job or something else will happen that I'll have to leave the Dominican Republic. There may come a time when I'll ask you and Iona for help. You are two of the most decent people I have ever met. I know I can trust you. Also, I like you both and want nothing bad to happen to you."

"Thank you," said Jeremy. "We have always liked you, too. You were the first person we contacted here because we knew we could trust you."

"Let's go," said Gavin. "Iona is expecting us."

They climbed up the stairs to the second floor with just enough light to see. A closed door with a big number 2 on the front led to the main hotel hallway. Opposite that doorway was a vent cover about 2 feet by 2 feet wide at the bottom of the wall. Gavin removed the vent cover and crawled into the duct. Jeremy followed. Crawling through the vent for about 20 feet, they came to another vent cover, and Gavin pushed it into the room. They both crawled in through the opening and into the bathroom. They entered the bedroom. Iona was sitting on the edge of the bed using the laptop that Gavin had provided her. She looked up, pushed the laptop onto the bed, and leaped into Jeremy's arms. She sobbed uncontrollably as she squeezed Jeremy as tightly as she could.

Jeremy and Iona embraced wordlessly, seemingly forever. Time seemed to stand still. After all that they had been through, and now they were together. They squeezed each other so tightly they could hardly breathe. They both had tears when the embrace relaxed, and they looked into each other's eyes. Nothing else in the world mattered. After a few minutes, they sat down on the bed.

"I would like to take you out of here tonight. Puerto Rico is 60 miles away, and we could be there on our boat by tomorrow night if we motor as fast as possible. We'll be safe there," said Jeremy. "They could replace the mast and fix the rigging. We could spend the rest of the season cruising in the Caribbean."

Iona thought about that for a minute. "There is more to the story than we know right now," said Iona.

"Someone has gone to a substantial amount of trouble to kidnap me and then remove one or both of my ovaries. It must be something to do with my hyper functioning T cells. I did some research on the Internet. They could find a functioning ovum and fertilize it with sperm from a male with similar functioning T cells. They could extract the T cells from the thymus at around 9 to 12 weeks. The embryonic T cells would be naïve. To put it another way, any human could use them to produce antibodies. Without the ability to produce missing antibodies, my embryo would die. I cannot let that happen."

"Maybe they could not retrieve an ovum. You are menopausal, so the number of usable eggs could be negligible," said Jeremy. "Maybe there is no embryo."

"Jeremy, I cannot leave until I know for sure," said Iona.

"How are we going to do that?" asked Jeremy.

"I don't know yet, but we've been through worse together," said Iona.

"There are contracts out to kill us on sight," said Jeremy. "They stacked the odds against us. It is going to be difficult."

Gavin sat while they discussed options and ideas. "I have an Airbnb close to here. I have not rented it at the moment. You two can use it. I rented it for next week, but it can buy you some time while you hide from these thugs."

Jeremy and Iona looked up at Gavin inquisitively.

"Nobody here knows about it. I had a little extra cash, and the opportunity came up, so I jumped in," Gavin stated. "The unit is self-sustaining and generates extra money monthly."

Iona smiled and asked, "Does this have anything to do with the 'Just ask for Gavin' that's all over social media?"

Jeremy looked at Iona. "What are you talking about?" He asked.

Gavin sighed and said, "It's a side business that generated a lot of extra cash. I never expected to have so much and to keep my money safe. I bought a condominium unit on Rincon Beach. I can't trust the banks. If things continue, I plan to buy another one next year."

Jeremy asked innocently, "How does 'Just ask for Gavin' generate money?"

"Honey, I will explain to you later," said Iona.

Changing the subject, Gavin said, "I do not think it is safe for you to stay here any longer. My suggestion is to stay at my Airbnb for the next few days. They are unlikely to find you there."

They discussed the plans. Just as they were getting ready to leave, they heard footsteps of heavy boots running in the hallway outside their room. Someone kicked the door in, and it fell into the room on its side. There were 3 men wearing balaclavas that stormed in from the hallways. The men carried pistols in their hands, and their eyes were madly darting around, looking for their targets. They came rushing into the bathroom, and finding no one, they continued to search the room. They checked under the bed and on the balcony. After 2 minutes of a fruitless search, they stormed out.

Gavin, Iona, and Jeremy watched the boots from inside the vent. Gavin had thrown the laptop computer into the vent system just as the assailants were kicking in the door from the hallway. They crawled in, and Gavin snapped the cover of the vent in place just as one man entered the bathroom. They remained motionless in the vent system to avoid making noise while the men searched for them. Once satisfied that the men had left, they quietly crawled through the vent system to the inner hallway. Upon arriving, they crawled out through the opening and into the dimly lit hallway.

Sitting on the stairs leading to the main floor in the dim incandescent light, they each took a big breath. They were safe….at least for now.

Chapter 36

There was an SUV following them. It was a 2-hour drive to the farmhouse where her family lived. Her oldest brother, Jose, was driving a Honda Civic. Jose was 35 years old and had a good job at the local supermarket. His job was to keep the food supply coming in to stock the shelves. It paid well by Dominican Republic standards, enough to pay for the car and give him a small apartment in Sousa. They were discussing the best way to get rid of the following car.

"There is a gravel road I will take up ahead." Said Jose. "It is quite twisty and dangerous for those unfamiliar with it. You might feel a little scared, but I have often driven on it. Trust me."

The Honda sped up to 100 k/hr. The SUV did the same and kept within 50 feet of the rear of the Honda.

"Hang on," cried Jose. Suddenly, he flipped the wheel to the right and sped up the gravel road in a cloud of dust. The SUV tried to do the same but missed the turn and ended up in the ditch. With the 2 minutes it took to extricate himself from the ditch, the driver sped up along the gravel road. They built the road into the side of the cliff of the mountain. Below the road, 100 feet almost straight down, was the blue Atlantic Ocean, with the surf crashing into the rocky shore.

The driver could see the Honda speeding along a few bends along the cliff, and he sped up to catch them. The driver was a seasoned professional, and his expertise was extracting information from those unwilling to give it to him. There would be few witnesses around when he rammed the back of the Honda to disable it. He would start with the man first and see what he knew. Women would often start talking when someone else was suffering to stop the torture. His instructions were explicit. Find out where Iona was hiding, and then kill them. His boss would be pleased.

The driver was now within 50 feet of the Honda. Jose sped up. He had a plan. The next turn was especially tight along the cliff, and he would take it at full speed. Just as he rounded the curve, he would slam on the brakes to avoid flying off the road into the ocean. There was an acute corner after the turn. He was hoping the SUV driver would follow him at full speed. The driver, not knowing about the tightness of the curve, would not have time to apply the brakes before he flew over the edge.

Jose took the corner at full speed, then slammed on the brakes. Sophie screamed, "We'll never make it!"

The car skidded close to the edge of the road. Sophie could see the white surf crash into the rocks 100 feet below. Just as she thought they would fly off the road, the controlled skid of the Honda had them back on the narrow road. Within 2 seconds, the SUV rounded the corner, flew silently over the edge of the road, and landed on the rocky shore below as if in slow motion. There was a loud crash as the SUV crumpled. Jose and Sophie left the Honda and silently looked at the wreckage. There was only the sound of the ocean breaking against the beach.

"We better get a move on," whispered Jose. Sophie could not move. She was in shock. Jose gently nudged her back into the car. They drove along the gravel road slowly until it met the main road. It took another 90 minutes to reach their destination. They traveled in silence as Sophie looked out the window pensively. She would have to talk to Iona about what happened. Iona would know what to do to help her work through the accident. She felt lucky to have Iona in her life. Her commitment to help Iona was more about saving herself, she thought. She would do anything for Iona,

The Honda pulled up to a house near where her family lived. Sophie recognized the farm as the one where her cousin lived. It surprised her to see her mother, father, and other brothers, sisters, and cousins there. She turned to Jose and said, "What's going on?"

"They know where we live. We are not safe going home, so we will stay here," said Jose.

Sophie got out of the car. She hugged her parents. Everyone was crying. They were so happy to see her after being away for over 2 years. The family hugged while they cried for Raphael, her youngest brother. They cried for Sophie, who was safe after surviving a hurricane. After 5 minutes, they pulled themselves together.

"We've got a pig roast for tonight," said Sophie's mom. "We'll be safe here. They may come for us, so we have moved out of the house until we figure out what to do. About 50 of the extended family are coming tonight because there is safety in numbers. The entire village is up in arms about what has happened to Raphael. Now, those evil men want to come after us because they think we know where Iona is hiding out. After everything Iona has done for you, we must protect her as if she is part of our family."

"Thanks, Mom," said Sophie. "We must use our strength in numbers to help Iona."

Over the rest of the evening, Sophie reconnected with her family. The roast pig was an immense success and would feed the extended family for at least another 2 days. There were laughs and tears during the encounters. Sophie recounted her adventure in the ocean with Jeremy. She shared her fondness for Iona and her commitment to doing everything she could to help her. The rest of her family was solidly behind her.

Just after sunset, 12 of the largest men of the family left the party to keep watch over Sophie's family farm. The rest of the family cleaned up after dinner and went to bed early. Some had to share beds, and some slept on the sofa. Others made temporary beds in the living room. Sophie smiled as she surveyed the family, coming together and supporting each other during difficult times. She went to sleep feeling safe. She fell asleep in less than a minute and drifted off, feeling happy.

Chapter 37

There were 10 of them quietly approaching the small house. The group's leader, Quan Wong, was an ex-military commander of the People's Liberation Army. Chinese investors in the pharmaceutical industry hired a private military group to protect their business interests abroad. There were over 40 of these para-military groups to choose from. They had chosen the group that was known for its brutality and stealth. A private security company called the Chinese Frontier Service Group protected foreign investments. They often operated outside of the law. The Chinese military had rejected these soldiers from the People's Liberation Army. Their inability to control their brutal and destructive attitude made them poor soldiers. These were the mercenaries that joined the Group. Starting salaries were 10 times what they could expect to make in the Army. The Group only hired those with a proven record of destructiveness. Huang Dong had chosen these 10 men that were selected to torture and then kill Sophie and her family once they got the information on Iona's whereabouts.

The clear night air allowed some light from the quarter moon directly overhead. The 10 mercenaries quietly and slowly approached the sleeping house along the gravel road. There was a car parked in front. Chickens were pecking at morsels of grains, and a thin wire fence surrounded them, preventing their escape. There was a gentle breeze coming from the sea. The only sounds in the night came from the chickens searching for food. The military trained the elite mercenaries to be so quiet they could get close enough to kill someone silently without detection. Hand signals were useless in the darkness, but each knew what to do.

Their weapons of choice were knives with razor-sharp edges, although they had their pistols with silencers strapped to their hips. They also carried grenades, smoke bombs and batons. One of them was a trained paramedic and carried ketamine and other drugs. They had effectively used Pentothal in the past to get information from noncompliant individuals. Then they would kill them. They were accountable only to Huang Dong, who instructed them to use any of their effective methods to get results. There was a $20,000 bonus if this mission was successful.

They planned to have 3 of them surround the house in case anyone escaped. 7 would quietly enter the house and spread out to cover the bedrooms. The mercenaries had studied the premises before the assault and knew some were sleeping in the same room. They would round them up and bring them into the living room. Their plans included tying them up and taking their time gathering information. One quality they shared was the pleasure of torture. The most satisfying part of any mission was when they could experiment with torture techniques to extract information.

For them, this was a straightforward assignment. This peasant farmer family did not stand a chance against such a well-trained team. The 10 of them had worked together in Rwanda to neutralize over 100 armed thugs who were trying to take over a diamond mine owned by a Chinese company. They slaughtered most of the poorly trained thieves. They tortured a few of the leaders until they died. One of the badly injured men escaped so his story could be told to dissuade others from trying something similar in the future. Tonight, Huang Dong instructed them to allow no survivors.

The 3 men assigned to watch the outside of the house spread out. The 7 men going inside the house gently stepped onto the wooden porch. Quan Wong quietly opened the door and stepped into the tiny living room. The others followed. There were 4 rooms where the family slept. Four of Quan's men simultaneously went into the rooms to round up the victims while Quan and 2 others waited with their knives in their hands in the living room. It was dead silent.

From the room on the right, there was a loud thud followed by a blood-curdling scream. One of the 2 mercenaries in the living room rushed into that room. Immediately, there was another loud thud followed by a similar blood-curdling scream. Quan peered into the room. He shone his light into the room. There was a bed along the far wall that was empty. There was a 4-foot by 4-foot hole in the wooden floor. At the bottom of what was a 10-foot-deep pit were the 2 men, where wooden spikes had impaled them. One man was still alive and looked up at him. His eyes were flashing, and he was trying to speak, but the spike went right through his chest, and all that came out was a whistling sound.

"Shit!" Quan cried out. "Let's get the fuck out of here!"

Screams were coming from the other 3 rooms as Quan backed out. He shone his light, which landed on the eyes of the remaining mercenary in the living room. The eyes betrayed fear as they darted from left to right. He was moving his body back and forth with the knife in his hand, looking for imaginary assailants to impale.

Quan briefly looked at the other rooms and saw similar holes in the wooden floors. At the bottom of each pit were the mercenaries impaled with wooden spikes. None were moving.

"Let's get out of here!" screamed Quan.

The remaining mercenary, followed by Quan, fled through the front door. As Quan exited, the severed head of the mercenary hit him with such force it knocked him onto the wooden porch. As he landed, there was a sharp pain in his right hand. Where the hand had been a few seconds earlier was only a stump. The severed hand was lying a few feet away. As Quan stared incredulously at the stump, he raised it to see the damage. It immediately soaked him in pulsatile blood, which got into his eyes. He could no longer see. Instinctively, he tried to wipe his eyes with the stump, which worsened the lack of vision. He began screaming, got up and ran down the gravel road. Tripping over the wire chicken fence, he landed among the startled chickens. He wiped his eyes with his good hand and saw a man standing over him with a machete.

"Get out of here," said Jose, the oldest brother of Sophie. "Tell your friends that we are coming after them. The rest of your team is dead. We will allow you to pick them up at the top of the driveway. If you do not pick them up within the next 12 hours, their pictures will be all over social media. Now go!"

Quan got up and started running down the driveway to the waiting van. He felt faint and was not sure if he would pass out. Draped over the steering wheel was the driver with his throat slit. Quan pushed him into the passenger's seat. He started the van and began driving to the lab. Feeling very weak, he knew if he tried to stand up, he would collapse. He parked in front and called Huang.

"There's been a problem," he said into the phone. "My men are all dead. I'm parked out front. I do not feel well…." The phone fell out of his good hand, and he slid down the driver's seat as he lost consciousness.

When Quan woke up, he was lying on a hospital gurney. The nursing staff had dressed the stump of the right hand with bandages. It was no longer bleeding. He had an intravenous with blood running into his left arm intravenous line. Huang was pacing the floor beside him in a rage, muttering to himself. As Quan opened his eyes, Huang turned to him.

"What happened?" Huang asked while trying to control his anger.

Quan recounted the entire narrative. It took about 10 minutes. Huang listened intently as Quan's quavering voice recounted in graphic detail the disastrous encounter. After Quan had finished the tale, he looked at Huang with fear in his eyes. Huang studied him. He slowly extracted his razor-sharp knife, and before Quan had time to react in the 3 seconds it took, his throat was slit. After 60 seconds, the gurgling from the open trachea subsided, and the body stopped twitching.

Chapter 38

Rachel was late. The cleaning started at 6 PM every night, and it would take the 3 cleaners until midnight to sweep and mop the floors. The bathrooms took about an hour each, and there were 4 of them. Luis, her 65-year-old uncle and one of the regular cleaners, had called her, saying one of the younger cleaners did not turn up. He wanted to know what he should do. There was no way the 2 remaining cleaners could finish on time. At midnight, the facility doors would automatically lock until 7 AM the following morning.

Rachel was 35 years old and had lived in the Dominican Republic for her entire life. Her husband had left her 3 years earlier and moved to New York, searching for a better life. The 3 small children she provided for as best as she could. She was grateful she had such a supportive family to help with the babysitting while she tried to scrape out a living.

A few years earlier, Rachel started a cleaning business with a steady supply of Airbnb, timeshares, and condominiums to clean once weekly. The hard part was finding cleaners who would only work Saturday or Sunday, as this was when the weeks typically change over. When the contract to clean the brand-new facility came up, offering steady employment every day, Rachel jumped at the opportunity. They needed the facility cleaned 7 days a week, but the one condition was they needed to be out of the facility by midnight. She had met with the one who appeared to be in charge, Huang Dong. He scared her. There was an icy calmness in his stare. He spoke with quiet authority. After the 2 interviews to get the contract, she left feeling he had threatened her if she failed to do a good job or was too nosy. He explicitly instructed me not to discuss with anyone what was happening there. Huang had said to her, "We wouldn't want anything to happen to your children, would we?"

There was only one way to interpret that threat, but she desperately needed the money.

On the night when they murdered Raphael, she was called at 6 AM to clean a 'chemical spill.' The usual cleaners would sleep at that hour, so she cleaned it herself. Immediately, she recognized the so-called chemical spill was blood. It was only later the same day that she found out they had murdered her cousin. When they threatened her cousin's family to keep quiet, she knew she would also have to keep quiet to keep her children safe.

Her cousin Sophie's return to the Dominican changed everything. Sophie had changed from the shy, complacent teenager when she left a few years ago to the feisty, organized woman of authority since she had been living in Canada. She seemed to be afraid of nothing. She quickly mobilized the extended family. There were at least 50 adult family members, ranging in age from 21 to 85.

Within a few hours, she convinced everyone they would be under attack and needed to prepare. No one believed her until the assault on the farmhouse. That they could fend off the well-trained militia surprised even the most skeptical of the family. This success empowered the entire family and bonded them in a way they had not felt for years.

Rachel rushed into the facility to help finish the cleaning before the midnight cut-off. Upon entering the building, she almost ran into Huang. "Watch where you are going," he yelled at her and then stormed into his office, slamming the door.

Rachel smiled. He had grossly underestimated the power of her extended family. They had agreed not to rest until they had destroyed the facility. There were a few staff remaining that evening. They were working on the benches, completing the day's work before leaving. Rachel knew she was practically invisible to the workers as she mopped the surrounding floor. The lab was mostly empty by 10 pm except for Huang. His light was on in his office. She cleaned the floor in the foyer in front of his office but was careful not to disturb him. She entered the adjacent office and began mopping the floor. When she got to the other side of the desk, she noticed the computer was on. Refilling the mop bucket in a utility closet, she checked on Huang, who was still busy in his office as she walked by.

She returned to the office that had the open computer. If she got caught by the psychopathic Huang, she knew he would certainly slit her throat. She clicked on the mail icon. Everything was in Mandarin. She typed in Sophie's email address. Rachel copied and pasted the IP address as Sophie had instructed her on the email subject line. She clicked send. She then deleted the email from the sent folder and returned the computer to the home screen. Rachel's pulse rate only settled down to normal when she returned to cleaning the rest of the office. The cold sweat that covered her forehead took a little longer to evaporate. By 11:45 PM, the 3 cleaners had completed their duties, and they left the facility together.

Chapter 39

Iona had wedged herself between Gavin and Jeremy on the 250cc Yamaha motorcycle. She had a helmet with a complete visor and could not see past Gavin, who was driving. Sitting behind her, Jeremy was hanging onto her waist, and she was hanging onto Gavin. When Gavin suggested the 3 of them take the motorcycle together to his Airbnb, her first thought was to stay at the hotel and take her chances with the hitmen. She thought 3 people on a small motorcycle was craziness until she saw a family of 5 wedged into the seat of a similarly sized motorcycle. The father was driving. The mother was at the back, keeping the children from falling off. They were going in the opposite direction from their motorcycle.

Arriving at the condominium complex at Rincon Beach, they placed the helmets on the motor seat. They had no luggage. The Airbnb was on the ground floor. It was a 2-story unit. The main bedroom was on the second floor, with a balcony looking out onto the beach. On the main floor was a medium-sized kitchen fully equipped with a dishwasher, oven, stove, fridge, microwave, and expresso machine. A sliding door opened to a private infinity pool that looked out over the beach. Gavin had fully stocked the fridge with fresh vegetables, milk, eggs, and other essentials. He had packed the freezer full of frozen meat and other foods.

"This will keep you going for the week," said Gavin. "I'll leave you the motorcycle. I better get back to work. I'll take an Uber. At 8 PM, expect a call from me." With that, Gavin stepped out of the condominium and headed for where the Uber would pick him up.

Sophie had contacted Jeremy earlier that morning using his new SIM card phone number. She recounted the massacre that had occurred at their farmhouse. The village had banded together to protect Sophie and her family. They stayed with friends nearby while others restored the house and cleaned the mess.

"Oh my God," said Iona after Jeremy told her what had happened. "I hope she is OK. After all the trauma she went through and all the psychotherapy, I hope she doesn't slip back into a deep depression."

"I'm no psychotherapist," quipped Jeremy. "But after the near-death experiences on the sailboat, I witnessed her resilience firsthand. A group of psychopathic militias won't send her back there. She seemed to suffer less psychological trauma than me after going through the hurricane."

Iona smiled. "She is a remarkable woman," said Iona.

"One of her cousins has a cleaning business, and the lab contracted her company to clean the facility," explained Jeremy.

"There was a computer left in one office last night, and the cousin emailed Sophie the IP address. Sophie hacked into the computer system and has been getting information. She is going to call us if she finds anything. Most of the research information is in Mandarin, but her program translates it into English immediately."

"Sophie doesn't appear to be going through any major PTSD at the moment," said Iona. "I hope it doesn't plague her later after all the excitement settles down."

"One of her biggest fears," said Jeremy, "is that something will happen to you. That is one of my fears, too. We are up against forces that are evil and corrupt."

"It is important for us to remind ourselves that there is more at stake than just our own lives," said Iona. "If something bad happens to us, it could adversely affect Sophie. Sophie has been effective at mobilizing her family. If that effectiveness slipped, her entire family may fall apart."

Jeremy thought about this for a moment. "We'll have to proceed carefully," he said. Jeremy was about to say something else when his cell phone chirped. "It's Sophie."

"Can I speak with Iona?" she asked Jeremy. Jeremy passed the phone to Iona.

"Iona, I am piecing things together. I hacked into the facility's system. It is difficult to understand the research jargon from the lab technician reports, but I accessed Huang's email. He encrypted many of the emails, but he sent one to someone I believe is his sister. Bragging about how well things are going, he claimed success will come soon. He mentioned they have a growing embryo that will soon be the key to curing cancer."

"Could you tell if that was my embryo he was referring to?" asked Iona.

"Further in the email, he mentioned he was particularly pleased because the ovum came from an older woman, and he was not sure it would work. I suspect that older woman is you, Iona."

"With that timeline, it makes sense that the embryo is mine," said Iona. "Raphael mentioned to me something about me being their only hope."

"Huang says that he is planning to move the facility to China. He mentioned some unforeseen developments in the Dominican Republic," replied Sophie. "He plans to freeze the embryo to make the transport safer. The team of 25 scientists, including a new scientist from Canada, a world authority in T cell extraction, would accompany him."

"Any idea when this will happen?" asked Iona.

"No mention of that, but I think it may be soon," answered Sophie. "We annihilated his team of commandos, and I suspect he doesn't trust his local hires as security guards. On the upside, we may be in a powerful position to retrieve the embryo as we have weakened his security forces."

"Even if we could retrieve the embryo, what would we do with it?" asked Iona.

"That is something we must think about," said Sophie. "In the meantime, let's work on a plan to get it out of their hands."

Iona went quiet for a few seconds while she thought about this before responding. "Let's talk later tonight. I need to discuss with Jeremy and think about what to do."

Jeremy pulled out the building plans Michael had sent to Sophie's email and said, "Michael sent me these to help find you. The detailed plans show the layout of the facility. The second floor is where they housed the laboratory. It looks like there is a spot for a freezer in this corner." Michael pointed to a spot on the floor plan. What we need to find out is where to find the incubator for the embryo."

"I wonder whether we could sneak into the facility tonight with Rachel disguised as cleaners?" asked Iona.

"Sounds too dangerous," said Jeremy. "They have cameras all over the place. They are on high alert, so unfamiliar faces would raise suspicions even if we tried to disguise ourselves. We could ask Rachel to take pictures and video to send us tonight."

They continued to discuss other ideas when Jeremy received a text message from an unknown number. "YOU NEED TO LEAVE NOW. THEY ARE COMING FOR YOU!"

Chapter 40

Li Ming was pacing in the hotel room. Bruce was fast asleep in bed. She wore him out after an afternoon of lovemaking. It was 8 PM. Things were unraveling quickly. Farmers eliminated the elite team of militia. After all the careful planning, how is that possible? She asked herself. Iona was on the loose, and that scared her. She had never encountered such a powerful woman. To have been so defiant and to escape from two very tough guards was not what she expected from a woman leading such a tranquil life. Li Ming needed to come up with a plan.

Her phone chirped. "Hello," she said.

"I know where Iona is hiding out," said the voice on the phone.

"Who is this?" asked Li Ming.

"My name is not important," said the voice. "I am one of the immigration officers. I also use Uber in my free time to make a few extra dollars. She is in an Airbnb on Rincon Beach with Jeremy. I do not know the number of the unit. When you get her, I want a bonus for giving you this information."

"How do I find the unit number?" asked Li Ming.

"You need to talk with Gavin, the manager of the marina. He is the one I gave a ride back to the marina. He left his motorcycle for them," said the voice.

"You talk to him!" retorted Li Ming. "We are 2 hours away. Iona is here in the country illegally. Do your job as an immigration officer and apprehend her. If you accidentally kill her because she is escaping, we'll pay you an extra $10,000. Take 2 of your coworkers and do your job. You'll be heroes, and you will also be $10,000 richer."

There was silence at the other end of the phone. "I'll call you after we have her," said the voice.

They arrived at the condominium complex at 9 PM. Gavin gave them the unit number. He was reluctant to divulge any information at first. A shoulder dislocation followed a few carefully planned punches to his pretty face. This caused his reluctance to divulge the information they wanted to evaporate. Gavin screamed in pain from the dislocated shoulder. "Unit 9A." he blurted out.

"You better be telling us the truth," said the immigration officer as they bolted. "We will come back for you if you are lying."

Gavin lay on the floor. Pulling out his cell phone with his good arm, he put it on the floor before him. He texted the message using his index finger. He pressed send. Then Gavin passed out.

The immigration officer had called 2 of his coworkers, who didn't take much convincing to help him. If they killed Iona, they would need to kill her husband as well. Jeremy was harboring an illegal alien and would naturally put up a fight. Killing them both could easily be justified. A bullet to each of their brains would allow the officers to take control of the situation.

The lights were on in the unit. They went to the beachfront and peered into the unit through the sliding doors. No one was there, but the light was on in the upstairs bedroom, where they were likely resting. They drew their guns, ready to pull the trigger, when they saw Iona. The leader of the group tried the sliding door. They had not locked the door. Idiots, he thought to himself. They deserve what is coming to them for being so careless.

He stepped inside. The others were right behind him. He made his way towards the stairs. There was a sudden tug on his left foot. He looked down, astonished to see a rope tight around his ankle. Before he could understand what was happening, the rope tightened, and he was hanging upside down from the chandelier. The gun flew out of his hand and landed on the kitchen floor. He screamed in pain as his ankle was now bent at 90 degrees, and all his weight was pulling on the fracture. The other two looked up at the dangling assailant just as Iona and Jeremy jumped off the top floor and landed on each of the remaining two officers. Their guns went flying out of the open sliding door into the infinity pool on impact. The startled officers stood up to face the jumpers. Iona kneed the first one in the groin. Using his momentum, she grabbed his right arm and twisted it at an unnatural angle as he fell out of balance. There was a loud crack as the bone fractured. A few seconds later, a blood-curdling scream came out from deep within his lungs.

Jeremy was facing the last assailant. He was the largest of the 3 men. He looked scared, having witnessed what had happened to his friends. His eyes were darting around the room as if looking for an escape. Iona quietly closed the sliding door to prevent it. He made a quick jab with his fist towards Jeremy, which missed but allowed Jeremy to land a powerful uppercut to the bottom of his jaw. There was a loud crack as the mandible shattered, and 3 teeth flew out of his mouth. He fell to the floor, unconscious.

The other two were whimpering. The one with the arm fracture tried to stand up, but Iona grabbed the arm and twisted it. He passed out in pain. Everything was over in less than 60 seconds.

Iona and Jeremy lowered the man from the chandelier and securely tied him up. They tied a gag around his mouth so he couldn't scream for help. They tied up the remaining two men together and gagged one of them. The man with the shattered mandible wouldn't be talking with such an extensive injury for a while. They were finishing up with the last ligature when Gavin hobbled in. His nose was bleeding. The swelling caused the left eye to stay shut. There was extensive bruising around the cheekbones. He was carrying his left arm in a homemade sling made from a sweater.

"Thank god you two are OK!" said Gavin. He was talking as if his mouth were full of marbles. Iona and Jeremy stared at him.

"What the hell happened to you?" asked Jeremy.

"These 3 guys beat the crap out of me," Gavin was pointing to them as he spoke. "They wanted the number of this unit. I held out as long as I could. I'm so sorry, I couldn't take any more. I'm so happy you are alive. What happened to them?"

"Thanks to your text message warning us. We were ready for them. We have some basic hand-to-hand combat training, and they were unprepared for that," Jeremy said.

"I grew up with these guys," said Gavin softly, "and I have worked beside them in the marina for 5 years. I never expected this from them. Money corrupts everyone and has changed what I thought were friends into brutal criminals. That's my fear of living here. Even when you do nothing wrong, there is always a fear that bad things will happen. It's fair to say that we can't trust anyone."

"That's not true," said Iona. "We trusted you, and it is because of us they have beaten you so badly." Iona and Jeremy had finished tying up the last two men who were still unconscious.

"Come into the bathroom and let me clean you up," said Iona. She softly touched his good arm and nuzzled him into the bathroom.

Jeremy heard the water running as he surveyed the damage. He knew they had to get out of the condominium. Jeremy made a phone call.

He was still on the phone when Gavin and Iona emerged from the bathroom. Gavin looked a little better, and Iona had cleaned the blood covering his face. His arm was out of the sling and hanging by his side. He had a crooked smile.

"Ok," said Jeremy to the phone, "Let me discuss with my team, but it sounds like a good plan."

"Iona replaced my dislocated shoulder," said Gavin. "I thought you told me she was a psychotherapist. It feels way better!" He moved his arm up and down, but his face winced with pain. "At least I can move it now."

"She has many talents. I, too, must remind myself not to cross her," said Jeremy, smiling as he pointed to the bodies around the room. "Let's go onto the veranda to talk. I just got off the phone with Sophie. She has a plan."

Chapter 41

Li Ming tried to call the number of the immigration officer who had spoken to her a few hours ago. There was no answer. After a few rings, the call went to voicemail. It was now approaching midnight. Something was wrong. Those immigration officers were idiots, she thought to herself. They had the advantage of surprise, yet somehow, they must have screwed it up.

Bruce was awake now. He was pecking on the keyboard of his computer. Immersed in his task, he was oblivious to the inner rage Li Ming was trying to control. He had told her earlier that he had some great new ideas for moving the project forward. What he was doing on the computer was a mystery to Li Ming, but she let him work undisturbed for the time being. She walked onto the balcony and closed the sliding door. She called Huang.

"I think they screwed it up," said Li Ming. "I tried to call, but it went to the voice mail."

"Those guys were useless to us," said Huang. "They didn't stand a chance against Iona. They have reduced the team to scientists and lab technicians. We have no one left we can trust as security. We need to move out tonight. I've called the entire team to come to the lab to get things packed up. We'll freeze the embryo and transport it that way."

"I'll meet you at the lab in 15 minutes," said Li Ming.

Li Ming walked back into the hotel room. "Honey," she said to Bruce, "There's a problem at the lab. We need your help. We need to go now."

Bruce seemed oblivious as she was talking to him as he was deeply immersed in his task on the computer. He kept banging away on the keyboard as if she wasn't there. Occasionally, he would grunt approval as if something on the computer screen pleased him.

"Bruce," she shouted. "We have a problem. We need to go."

There was still no response from Bruce. She had experienced his transcendent behavior in the past, and usually, she could wait until he finished with what he was doing, but tonight, there was no time.

"Bruce!" she screamed. "We need to go!" She walked up to the laptop and slammed the computer shut. "There is a problem at the lab. We could lose everything unless we shut it down tonight!"

Bruce stared up at her. He felt fear running through his body. He had never seen her like this before. The rage coming from her was something he had witnessed only from his coworkers at the lab in Toronto when he had said something that displeased them. He had only experienced tenderness from Li Ming. She was hyperventilating, and her face was bright red. There was a nervous tic, causing her right eye to blink repeatedly. Bruce could feel her laser-focused rage directed at him through her pinpointed pupils. For the first time, Li Ming scared him.

He opened his mouth to speak, but no words came out. Standing, he felt faint and had to sit down. He stared at her.

Recognizing his discomfort, she seemed to soften. "The driver is waiting for us downstairs," she whispered. She reached over and touched his face. A tear rolled down his cheek. For Bruce, it was as though something beautiful had died. He had never experienced passion before. No one had paid any attention to him before. He had been alone for so long before Li Ming entered his life. This must be what people with a substance use disorder feel when their supply gets cut off, he thought. It was as though he had been living in a dream for the past 6 months. In a flash, he knew it was over.

In Bruce's world, things were black, or they were white. There was no middle ground. By watching movies and talking to coworkers, he knew relationships go through difficulties. He could never understand what they were talking about. When someone asked him for advice, which was rare, on some minor relationship infraction, he would tell them to get rid of their partner. No one ever took his advice, and he never understood why.

The moment passed as quickly as it came, but for Bruce, everything had changed. He stood up and followed Li Ming into the hallway, the elevators, and the waiting car. They drove to the laboratory. It was after midnight when they arrived. Li Ming used her passkey to let them in. They walked up to the second floor and into Huang's office. The door was open. They sat in the 2 chairs opposite Huang.

Li Ming thought Huang would be in a rage, given all that had happened in the past 24 hours, but he seemed strangely calm. Maybe it was because he decided to close the lab, and they could move forward.

"Hello, Bruce," he said. "Thanks for coming. We are closing the lab. The plan is to continue the research in China. They have a similar lack of scrutiny over this research so that we can continue. We will provide everything you need to make the project successful."

Bruce stared at him. He looked over at Li Ming, who appeared to look at him with those soft, large, and adoring eyes. She sighed and leaned her head against his shoulder. He continued to stare at Huang.

"We have great things ahead for us," said Huang. "We are on the cusp of the best advance of cancer care ever in the history of medicine."

Li Ming said, "Bruce is a little overwhelmed at the moment. Let's go to the lab. Bruce, you can show us what we will need for the next steps." Li Ming gently stroked his arm. He looked down at her hand with no emotion.

They got up to leave, but Bruce remained sitting.

"Bruce," said Li Ming quietly, "Are you coming?"

Bruce looked up at them. They were standing beside each other. Huang looked confused, not sure what to say. Li Ming seemed to get agitated. She was gradually transferring her weight from the left foot to the right.

"I'm not going with you," said Bruce. "I'm going back to Toronto. Count me out!"

Bruce got up to leave and started walking towards the door. Huang said, "Bruce, do not do this. We need you!"

Bruce continued to walk away. Huang pulled out his razor-sharp knife and approached Bruce as he was walking away. Stunned, Li Ming watched as the disaster unfolded before her eyes. She stared, horrified, not wanting to believe what would happen. Unable to stop herself, she shouted, "No!" loudly. Bruce stopped and turned around just as Huang was about to slit his throat. He stepped to the side with a shocked look and put up his arm to protect his neck. Suddenly, the lights went off. The sounds of the air conditioner stopped. There was a complete power failure. Bruce felt the knife slice into his forearm. He fell to the floor in complete darkness and rolled away from where he thought Huang might be. He quietly stood up and turned to where he remembered the hallway was located.

Bruce scampered away into the darkness, feeling lucky to be alive.

Chapter 42

Sophie could see the drama unraveling from her laptop. She was in the back seat of her brother's car and could see the facility from her vantage point 100 feet away. Gavin sat beside her, ready to help when they needed him. She had hacked into the security system and accessed the facility's cameras. There was a lot of activity in the lab. They appeared to be packing things in boxes and loading the boxes onto the trucks waiting at the rear of the facility.

She was uncertain as to the location of the embryo but had narrowed it down to 3 areas. She had seen one of the lab technicians take a test tube and drop it into a square container of what she assumed was liquid nitrogen. Steam was coming from the top of the container before the lab technician screwed the lid on tightly. She then placed the container into a silver portable freezer. It was here that Sophie suspected they housed the embryo.

Sophie was about to call Jeremy on his cell phone to update him on her findings. Everyone was in position. Sophie saw Li Ming and another man, likely Bruce, enter the facility. She watched them walk to the second floor and sit in Huang's office. There was a conversation, but Sophie only had access to the images and could not hear what they said. When the man she thought was Bruce stood up and started walking away, Huang pulled out his knife. It took her 5 seconds to turn off the power grid. Her screen went black. She had turned off the backup generator earlier in the evening, so the auxiliary power system did not kick in. She could not be certain, but she hoped she was just in time.

"Jeremy," she said into her phone, "I had to cut the power sooner than planned. Huang was about to slit Bruce's throat. I think they argued. I hope I was fast enough."

"No worries, we are all in position, ready to go inside," said Jeremy.

Sophie explained to Jeremy where she suspected they had stored the embryo. She described the dismantling of the laboratory benches and the transport of boxes to the trucks. "There was no sign of any security, just the researchers and the lab assistants. There must be 25 of them."

Jeremy, Iona, and 10 of Sophie's brothers and cousins slowly entered the facility through the front door. They had headlights that shone a powerful beam ahead of them. They made their way up the stairs and to the laboratory bench area. Most staff packing the equipment in boxes had fled because of the power failure. They were now milling around the rear of the building around the trucks, not understanding what had happened. Power failures were part of daily life in the Dominican Republic, and they were prepared for that. The generator had always kicked in before tonight. Many assumed it would just be a few minutes before they could return to work.

The team of Iona and Jeremy found themselves in front of the portable freezer, where they suspected they housed the embryo. It took 2 of the strongest of Sophie's brothers to lift it. They carried it out the front door and into a van owned by one cousin.

Jeremy, Iona, and the others remained behind in the lab. They needed to check a few other areas to avoid leaving without the embryo. There was a small room next to the main laboratory. Jeremy and Iona entered the room.

A bench was on the far wall. Two glass containers had tiny tubes entering from the top. There was a battery-powered pump that circulated the fluid into the glass containers. Jeremy and Iona approached the bench and shone their lights into the glass containers.

"Oh my God," exclaimed Jeremy. "As ridiculous as it sounds, I think we found your ovaries!"

"And look!" said Iona, "If I weren't a psychotherapist, I would say that this one contains a testicle! I wonder how they got that."

"What do you think we should do?" asked Jeremy.

Iona looked at Jeremy. She had imagined what she might do if she encountered such Frankenstein-like projects in this laboratory. There was no way she would leave them to repeat the illegal experiments they had created with the embryo. The thought of returning the testicle to the rightful owner occurred to Iona, but finding who that was in a timely fashion would not be possible. The ovaries were from her. She had no further use for them. In her mind, because they were rightfully hers, she could dispose of them any way she wished. She hoped that the owner of the testicle had similar sentiments.

Iona felt strangely in control. A family of a deceased African American woman had tested the ethics of conducting research on someone's tissue without permission. Henrietta Lacks died of cervical cancer in 1951. They took a sample of her cells without her permission. They gave them to a researcher called George Gey. Normally, human cells can only multiply and divide a fixed number of times. The cancer cells continued to multiply and divide indefinitely. These HeLa cells, named after the deceased woman, revolutionized cancer research. Dr. Gey supplied HeLa cells to international researchers, and thousands of patents resulted. It has saved millions of lives. They gave no acknowledgment to Henrietta Lacks or her family. Because of this case, most countries have laws about informed consent and privacy with patient's tissue. They made the rules to protect patients and their families.

Iona knew what she was going to do.

"Ooops," she cried out. She swept the glass containers and their battery-powered pumps onto the floor with her left arm. There was a loud crash as the glass shattered and the fluid spread across the linoleum. The preserved gonads slid across the floor into the corner and rested against the wall. The pumps stopped working.

"An experiment with my body parts is now over," said Iona triumphantly. "I have been waiting for this moment!"

"Let's get out of here," said Jeremy. They gathered up the remaining team members and headed for the door. Jeremy took the rear to make sure they left no one behind. Just as he was almost at the door, he felt a prick in his neck. He focused intently on getting through the door but stumbled. His consciousness slipped away. He fell to the floor. Before losing consciousness, he looked up to see Li Ming and Huang looking down at him. Then blackness.

Chapter 43

When they reached the van, the other cousins were waiting for them. Sophie was there with Gavin. It excited them that the extraction was a success. They had done what they had planned, and there were no hitches.

Iona hugged Sophie. She turned around, looking for her husband. "Sophie, have you seen Jeremy?" Iona asked.

Sophie looked around. "I thought he was with you," she said.

"He was right behind me when we left the building," Iona said.

"Let me call him on his cellphone. I'll put him on the speakerphone. He'd better have a good excuse for not being with us," Sophie said as she pressed his number. On the second ring, the phone was answered. "Jeremy, where the heck are you?"

There was a stony silence on the other end of the line. "This is Li Ming. We have Jeremy with us. You can only get him back if you return the embryo. We want Iona to come back into the facility. I'll send the truck to your van. Your boys can load the freezer containing the embryo onto the truck." The line went dead.

Iona looked at Sophie. "There is no way they are getting my embryo. That is a piece of me and belongs to me. No one can take that away from me."

Iona went quiet. "I need to think for a moment." She sat down on the curb and put her head in her hands. They were almost successful. They must have captured Jeremy at the last moment. The sedation was probably the same stuff they gave me, she said to herself. An idea sparked in her mind.

"Sophie, take the embryo out of the freezer and keep it safe. We'll load the freezer onto the truck as they have asked us, but without the embryo. I'm going back in to rescue Jeremy. They probably hit him with a huge dose of ketamine, so he'll be out for hours. Call that number and say we want proof that Jeremy is alive."

Sophie dialed Jeremy's number. "Before we agree on anything, we need proof he is alive," said Sophie. "Send us a video."

Less than a minute later, Sophie received a text message. There was a video of Jeremy on the floor. They tied his hands behind his back. A large boot came from the right of Jeremy and kicked him in the stomach. There was a soft groan that came from Jeremy. A voice said, "If you want more proof, I can kick him in the face and rearrange his nose. Otherwise, do as I say!"

Sophie called him back, "OK, we'll load the freezer onto the truck. Iona is on her way in through the front door."

"If I am not out in 10 minutes, send in the cousins with their machetes," said Iona as she walked away.

Sophie stepped into the van. Her eldest brother shone a light into the freezer, and they pulled out the square container housing the glass tube with the embryo. Using a pair of tongs, Sophie reached into the liquid nitrogen and pulled out the glass tube. She laid it in a clean towel and wrapped it up to keep it frozen as long as possible. She hoped Iona would come back quickly.

Sophie screwed the lid onto the liquid nitrogen container and placed it back into the portable freezer. She carried the towel wrapped around the test tube containing the embryo to her brother's car and sat in the passenger's seat. She would protect the embryo as if it were her child growing. Sophie felt a tear running down her cheek. If Iona could be so brave, why couldn't she?

She knew she had to pull herself together. She reminded herself of what she had told Jeremy at sea. 'Hell hath no fury like a woman scorn.' They had killed her youngest brother, and they had tortured Iona. Someone was going to pay.

Iona opened the front door of the facility and walked up the stairs. Jeremy was lying against the wall, tied up. They must have dragged him up the stairs, thought Iona. Li Ming and Huang were standing over him. They turned to face her. A battery-powered exit light in the hallway provided just enough light to make out their faces.

"You do not know how much damage you have caused," said Huang. "The consortium of Chinese pharmaceutical companies has invested hundreds of millions into the project. The only thing left is the embryo, loaded onto the truck as we speak. Both you and Jeremy will pay for the harm you have caused us with your lives."

Huang pulled out his knife. "You have witnessed firsthand the damage I can inflict with this." He thrust the knife into the air. "I am going to enjoy slitting your throat. I needn't bother with Jeremy because this building will blow up in 4 minutes and 30 seconds with what I leave of you and Jeremy inside."

Huang approached Iona with the knife in his right hand. Iona thought back to hand-to-hand combat training and looked for the clues the commander had taught her to find. There was a coldness in his eyes that betrayed no emotion. She could not see clues that would determine if he would feint to the left or right. She anticipated he would come directly at her and mentally prepared for that. He was a professional, unlike the last group of immigration officers she and Jeremy had disabled. They were clumsy and had no training in what they were trying to do. Huang was a seasoned killer. She began to harbor doubt about whether she knew enough to stop him from killing her.

Huang lunged at her. She stepped to the right and, with the back of her left hand, knocked the knife out of Huang's right hand. He was faster than she had expected and grabbed her arm with his left hand, using her forward momentum to spin her around. He had her in a death-grip neck hold. She couldn't breathe. He held on so tightly she couldn't employ the techniques they had taught her to break his grip. Her legs were flying madly in the air. She felt faint.

Bruce watched the drama unfolding from his position crouched down on the 3rd step of the stairs. The light was just enough to see them. At first, he ignored what was happening between Huang and Iona. He focused on Li Ming. She was standing with her arms crossed, staring at the two struggling. A satisfied grin was on her face, as if she was happy that Huang was about to kill Iona. He had never witnessed that part of Li Ming. He felt confused and betrayed. Until this trip, Li Ming had always treated him with kindness and tenderness. She seemed fascinated by his superior intellect. His social awkwardness, which he had struggled with all his life, didn't matter to her.

Now, she had become like everyone else. When Huang attacked him just before the lights went out and he was ready to slice him up, she didn't try to stop him. She just yelled, "No!". It seemed to Bruce that the sound came out involuntarily before she could stop it.

The research facility lacked the necessary ethical structure for quality research. Without proper ethical guidelines, the research facility's results would not be accepted by the scientific community. From Bruce's familiarity with rigorous checks and balances in research, he knew this project would be a waste of time. If it became public, this facility would delay his life's work for years and throw a skeptical shadow on his accomplishments. Bruce felt an anger rise in his chest that he had never felt before. They tried to trick him. Li Ming, all along, had been using him to get him to agree to be part of this madness. He stood up. It was as if he had lost his ability to control what he was about to do. He felt as if he was looking down from above at himself, unable to control his movements.

Out of the darkness, Bruce appeared. He was running right at the struggling Iona and Huang, yelling at the top of his lungs. His pudgy 250-pound body slammed into the Iona and Huang. Iona flew out of the death grip and onto the floor, somewhat dazed. Bruce found himself lying on top of Huang. "You bastard! You were going to kill me all along!" Bruce was pounding Huang in the face until it became a bloody mess. After 15 seconds, Huang stopped moving.

Bruce stood up to face Li Ming. Her facial expression had changed. She looked scared. Bruce knew she had never witnessed him in one of his rages before. When the rages occurred in the past, they were usually rants about some minor differences of opinion with his colleagues. This was different. Bruce had never physically assaulted anyone before today. The violence frightened him as well. He stared at Li Ming, not knowing what would happen next. Li Ming stared back at him. Her eyes betrayed her fear. They were darting up and then down as if trying to anticipate his next move. She didn't say anything. She was shifting her weight from her left foot to her right. Bruce recognized that this was what she would do when she got nervous.

Suddenly, Li Ming turned around and fled into the darkness of the lab. Bruce could hear her footsteps fade as she ran into the depths of the dark and empty lab. A door slammed. Then there was silence.

Chapter 44

Jeremy was still stuporous when the first explosion shook the ground. They positioned him against a building across the street, sitting with his back against the wall. Iona draped herself over him as if to protect him from the blast. The explosion sent a plume of dust and debris into the night sky, raining down on them. He pushed Iona over and protected her body with his as he was now awake. Another explosion about 30 seconds after the first one sent another round of dust and debris into the sky. It was raining down on them again. There was a loud rumble as the facility collapsed into rubble.

The dust and small pieces of gravel covered Iona and Jeremy. When a quiet atmosphere prevailed, they shook off the dust and stood up. They stared at the remains of the facility. Only the foundation remained along with one wall. Small fires and sparks from exposed electric wires were on the ground level. The second floor, where Jeremy had lain unconscious only minutes before the explosion and where they left Huang, was gone. It had collapsed, taking the entire lab with it. Gone were all the lab benches, freezers, and other equipment.

The building was too unstable to go looking for survivors. It might take weeks to dig out the bodies of Bruce and Huang from the rubble. The explosion would have blown them to bits, and the fires would burn them to be unrecognizable. It was possible they could not identify which charred remains belonged to which person.

"How did you get me out?' asked Jeremy.

Iona told him how Huang and Li Ming sedated him as he was leaving and how she went back in to rescue him.

"Bruce came out of nowhere and beat Huang into a pulp," explained Iona. "He helped me drag you out of there. Huang told me they had rigged the building with explosives in case they needed to leave in a hurry. We knew we only had a few minutes before the time would run out. After laying you down here, Bruce took off into the building. I think he went looking for Li Ming. He ran in just before the building collapsed. I cannot see how he would have survived."

Sophie came rushing up to them. "Thank God you are OK. Everyone in my family is safe," said Sophie. "I have accounted for everyone, but we were worried about you two."

"We are fine," said Iona. "What is happening with the embryo?"

"The solution unfortunately thawed," said Sophie. "There is no way we can get it into a freezer again. The freezer and liquid nitrogen are gone. I do not know what we should do."

Iona and Jeremy sat on the sidewalk to think about what to do. "Let me call the Chief of Obstetrics and Gynecology, Andre Rockman, at the Metropolitan hospital," said Jeremy. "He'll know what we should do."

Jeremy and Andre had been friends from medical school. They had been crewing on a sailboat for weekend races in Lake Ontario to escape the rigors and stress of medical school. It was a time they both reflected on fondly whenever they met. Andre had done his obstetrics and gynecology training in Montreal. It was a pleasant surprise for them to work at the same hospital after finishing their residency. Andre had largely given up sailing because his wife would get seasick when the boat left the dock. However, Andre never refused an invitation from Jeremy and Iona to accompany them on a weekend sail.

They remained friends, although their relationship had chilled over the past year. Jeremy tried not to think about his last medical advisory meeting over one year ago when his friend Andre had not supported him when he needed it most. While left stranded trying to defend an important issue by himself, Andre did not jump in to defend him.

Jeremy called the hospital, who patched him through to Andre's cellphone. It was 2 in the morning, but being an obstetrician, Jeremy thought he would be used to getting his sleep disrupted. Andre picked up on the third ring.

"Hi, Andre, this is Jeremy Young."

There was silence on the other end. Jeremy wasn't sure if he had hung up at the sound of his voice. Jeremy had not spoken to him for over a year, so he did not know if Andre was harboring ill feelings towards him.

"Hello, Andre?" he asked into the phone.

"Sorry, Jeremy, it's been a long time. I wasn't expecting a call from you. Where are you?" asked Andre.

"I'm in the Dominican Republic. I was hoping you could give me some advice," said Jeremy. He explained about the embryo and asked, "Do you have any thoughts on how we might save it?"

"Jeremy, that is a wild story you just told me," said Andre. "As you know, we have one of Toronto's most advanced infertility clinics. To give you a little background, the funding came from an anonymous source 2 years ago. I have been beating myself up for not supporting you when you ran into trouble last year. After everything you have been through, I hope you can forgive me. We have been friends for a long time."

"Not to worry about that, Andre," replied Jeremy. "It's all water under the bridge. I wouldn't be calling you if I didn't trust you."

"Ok," said Andre. "You must put the embryo in a safe place. The safest place is inside the uterus. You would need to find a woman in the fertile age range. She would need to be 8 to 10 days post ovulation. You must transfer the embryo in the next 2 hours for the best chance of success. To transfer the embryo into a surrogate uterus is the easiest part." Andre explained to Jeremy how to do it.

"Thanks, Andre. That is good advice. I'll let you know what we decide to do. We'll be sure to get together when I return to Toronto." Jeremy hung up the phone.

Iona and Jeremy discussed how best to manage the thawed embryo. One option would be to let the embryo die. Just talking about that option caused a teardrop to run down Iona's cheek. "That is a piece of me. I must do whatever I can to save it."

"What if we ask Sophie to be the surrogate?" asked Jeremy.

"That is completely out of the question," replied Iona. "That would violate every single patient/therapist boundary imaginable. Even if she offered to do that, we would have to refuse to let her. Patients develop trust with their therapist, and many patients would do anything the therapist asks. Rational thought evaporates. The risk of damage to Sophie after everything she has been through would be too great."

"Maybe one of her extended family could do it? Or perhaps a friend?" suggested Jeremy. "We have to act fast, though."

Iona reluctantly agreed to talk with Sophie to see if she knew anyone who might act as a surrogate. They went to look for her. Her brother's car was gone. Some of her cousins were milling around the destroyed facility, but none knew where she was. Jeremy tried calling her cell phone, but it went to voicemail. He called the oldest brother, but his voicemail picked up the call. Iona and Jeremy were getting worried about what might have happened to Sophie when the car arrived. Sophie got out and gave them each a hug.

"Jeremy spoke to a fertility expert in Toronto," said Iona. "He suggests we find a surrogate uterus to see if it grows to term. Do you know anyone? We will pay for all expenses. Perhaps one of your cousins, or do you have a friend?"

Sophie began to cry. Her sobs became louder and louder.

"What's the matter, honey?" asked Iona softly. "Has something happened to the embryo?"

Sophie nodded her head. "I'm sorry, Iona. I knew I had to act quickly. I also knew that you would never allow me to be the surrogate. I looked up how to transfer the embryo into a uterus online. I had our local family doctor transfer the embryo to me. Please forgive me." Sophie burst into tears again.

Iona wrapped her arms around her and cried with her. Jeremy stared at the two of them as they sobbed uncontrollably and smiled. Sophie was going to make the best mother any child could want.

Chapter 45

There was a soft breeze from the east, the same direction they were motoring. It was pitch black outside, as clouds were covering the sky. It was a warm night, and they were making good time with the 80-hp diesel engine going 8.5 knots. Iona and Jeremy were in the cockpit of their sailboat talking. Being too wound up, they could not sleep. It had been a harrowing 24 hours, but they felt they were through the worst.

"Michael wanted us to call him," said Iona. "He said it didn't matter if it was late."

"Now is probably a good time," said Jeremy as he picked up his cell phone and dialed Michael's number. Michael answered on the first ring.

"Jeremy," said Michael, "Is everything OK?"

"We left a few hours ago," said Jeremy. "We are 12 miles off the coast and heading directly for San Juan."

"Someone from the Canadian consulate will meet you when you arrive at the government dock, a fellow called James Robinson," said Michael.

"We should be there sometime around 10 AM the day after tomorrow," said Jeremy. "We'll call the cellphone number you gave us when we get closer."

"Good luck and stay safe," said Michael as he ended the call.

Jeremy looked at Iona as he hung up the phone and said, "Why don't you try to get some sleep? It's going to be a long night. I'll get you up in 3 hours, and you can relieve me."

Iona was about to object when a wave of overwhelming fatigue hit her. She went down the companionway, past the aft bunks where the others were sleeping, and into the forward bunk. There were enormous waves, and the forward bunk was bouncing wildly. Iona crawled into bed, and despite the erratic movements of the boat, she passed out in seconds.

Jeremy, still too wound up to sleep, thought about the escape from the Dominican Republic. Within 20 minutes of the first explosion, there were police and fire trucks everywhere. Iona, Jeremy, Sophie, and her family team quietly left the wreckage after the building collapsed. Some team members were in Jose's Honda, and others had been driven away in the van. The rest of them walked through the deserted back streets to avoid detection, unaware of their next move. The general plan was to get back to the cousin's farm and figure things out. Out of nowhere, a black SUV appeared. They all began running down the narrow street as the SUV pulled up beside Jeremy.

"Jeremy," said a familiar voice. "It's me, Ray, from CSIS. Stop running!"

Jeremy stopped in his tracks. He peered through the open window and recognized Ray and his partner.

"What the hell are you doing here?" asked Jeremy. "You told me you don't get involved with international affairs."

"Hop in," said Ray. "We need to talk."

Iona and Sophie walked over to the SUV. Jeremy quickly explained to Sophie who the men were, and the two women hopped into the SUV together. The 3 of them were sitting on the bench behind the front seats.

"We saw this was developing into a shit show," said Ray. "Our boss told us this was our mess to clean up and to head down here. What happened tonight will no doubt result in international repercussions. China has already denied involvement. There are dead bodies, a blown-up facility, and immigration officers badly beaten up. They sent us down here to see what we could do for damage control."

Jeremy, Iona, and Sophie sat solemnly and listened. The remaining members of Sophie's family were sitting on the curb. Two vehicles emerged from the darkness and came down the street behind the black SUV. One of Sophie's cousins knocked on the window.

"Sophie," he said, "Jose and the van are arriving to bring us home. What do you want to do?"

Ray said, "I can drive them wherever they wish, but I'd like to speak with them first. Is that OK?"

Sophie nodded after Jeremy and Iona approved. "OK, we'll catch up with you in a little while," she said.

"We need to get you out of here," said Ray. "The immigration officials are going to be looking for you. The 3 that visited you earlier this evening claim Iona is here illegally, and when they went to arrest her, they got beaten up. We believe they will try to pin the deaths of the ex-military Chinese military on you two as well. You might be in jail for a long time. The deaths getting blamed on Canadians may well cause further strains on Canada-Chinese relations. This is something the Canadian government wishes to avoid. The diplomatic fallout could cause irreversible economic repercussions.

"We've been following the drama on our high-resolution satellite cameras, but it only gives us part of the picture, so we hope you can fill in the blanks for us."

Jeremy recounted the events to date. He summarized the story in 15 minutes, highlighting the main points. Ray pulled out his notepad and made notes.

Jeff, the other CSIS agent who had been quiet until this point, spoke. "If we could get you out of the country tonight, they might blame everything on an illegal drug operation. They would sweep the deaths of the militia under the rug. This security force often takes contracts for drug operators to protect their out-of-country assets."

Jeremy, Iona, and Sophie thought about this for a moment. "We cannot leave without Gavin," said Sophie. "They beat the crap out of him and will accuse him of assisting an illegal alien, Iona. What can we do about him?"

Ray and Jeff went silent. "We can't help him. Our mandate is to protect Canadians. He's going to have to fend for himself."

An idea flashed through Jeremy. "Let me call Michael. I remember him explaining something to me two years ago. When Sophie had her issues, he explained the Canadian government would readily accept those refugees who may be in danger in their own country. Let me call him.”

Jeremy hopped out of the car for privacy. He did not want the 2 spies to hear what he would say confidently to his lawyer. After a 10-minute conversation, he hopped back in the car and said, “Let’s go to Sophie’s cousin’s farm and talk with Gavin. Michael is going to see what he can do.”

Jeremy smiled to himself from the cockpit of his sailboat. The mast was gone from his beautiful boat, so that he couldn’t sail, but he was happy and felt safe. They were out on the open ocean, and it was unlikely radar could detect him, as the boat was only 5 feet above sea level without the mast to act as a radar beacon. Anyone within range using radar could easily interpret the boat as a wave. Iona, Sophie, and Gavin were all sleeping in their cabins, now safe from the reach of the corrupt Dominican Republic officers. Although they were not completely out of danger, they were heading in the right direction. For the first time in weeks. Jeremy felt in control.

Chapter 46

The sun was beating down on the luxury superyacht. The enormous umbrella fixed on the transom of the boat prevented sunburn. An orange-colored drink rested on the coffee table beside the cushioned lounge chair. A server arrived and asked if there was anything else he could do, but a single shake of the head was all the server needed to know not to be of any bother. They would anchor for the night within the next hour. Thailand was probably the most beautiful cruising ground on the face of the earth. It was also where many people who had a past to hide lived. Few countries had extradition agreements. Few people in Thailand even cared about anyone's past as long as they spent their money there.

Li Ming smiled as she sipped her cold drink. It had been too easy. Huang had transferred the million dollars promised to Bruce for extracting the T cells from the embryo. Bruce's promise of long-term employment resulted in an extra 5 million being transferred to an intermediary private bank account. Li Ming had transferred the money to her bank account.

She had convinced Huang that the transfer was necessary to prove to Bruce they were serious about him working for them. Huang had inadvertently blown Bruce to bits before she could show him. The last time she saw Huang, he was unconscious after being beaten to a pulp. The building explosion happened 2 minutes after she saw him lying on the floor in a pool of blood. He undoubtedly blew himself to bits along with Bruce.

Everyone who could harm her was dead. She had grown quite fond of Bruce after spending so much time with him. Given his background as a researcher, it was not surprising that he would feel guilty and have doubts about working illegally on embryos. It could not have worked out in the long term for them as a couple. Li Ming wanted only one thing from Bruce, and he had given it to her. A life of luxury. She smiled as she thought about how great things had worked out.

Her relationship with Huang was more complex. He was a psychopath, taking pleasure in controlling people and then killing them. She knew that when Huang had no further use for her, he would kill her as well. Getting blown to bits by the explosives he had planted reflected the irony that was fitting for someone as evil as Huang. Just thinking about how lucky she was to have him out of the picture brought a smile to her face.

Yacht rentals were cheap in Thailand. $10,000 bought her food, drinks, a server, and a yacht with a captain for the next month. She needed time to plan for her next venture. There were plenty of available wealthy men she could entrap and then embezzle. She knew men found her attractive, and she knew how to manipulate them. She also knew she was smart. Before they could understand what happened, she would have them transfer a fortune to her. Although she could happily live on the money she had stolen that should have belonged to Bruce, she needed excitement. Playing with men's desires brought her that excitement.

The yacht engine slowed as the captain pulled up to a protected spot to lower the anchor. The boat stopped, and the captain dropped the anchor in 30 feet of water. He reversed the engines to set the anchor, then turned off the motor. The sun was about to set. Li Ming looked at the sunset and sighed. She reflected on how far she had come since that first visit from Huang to her university. Now, she had set herself up for life. Life was good.

Li Ming watched as the captain and server lowered the dinghy into the water. They had to run into town for some last-minute supplies for dinner. Fresh vegetables and fruits made eating on board a pleasure. Dinner would be at 8 PM, they told her. She saw them speed away towards the shore as she closed her eyes. A quick nap before dinner would be welcome. She drifted off to sleep in the warm, fragrant breeze coming from the land.

When the luxury yacht exploded, the entire sky lit up. The 10,000 liters of fuel burned for about 15 minutes as the boat sank in the harbor. Huang witnessed the entire process from his vantage point on the dock. Placing explosives on the hull was easy. Detonating them from a safe distance was easier. Li Ming was the last piece of the project to be buried. The project was dead in the water. It turned out that T cells were not the answer to cure cancer that everyone in the consortium was hoping for. It worked sometimes, and survival rates from cancer had improved, but it did not work for everyone. There were still many questions about cancer to answer, and a cure was nowhere in sight.

Huang sighed, then turned around and walked away. He would look for other projects when he got back to China. He had some leads on weapon deals, which would be a better fit for his personality.

Chapter 47

The choice for the Nobel Prize for medicine that year was straightforward. Raphael was 20 years old when he defended his PhD, where he proved he had discovered the cure for cancer. No one had seen such a brilliant mind at such a young age before. Curing cancer involves prevention from a young age, long before cancer develops. The simplest way to think of it was to compare it to vaccines given to children to prevent hepatitis or pneumococcal meningitis. The answer, of course, was a lot more complicated than that.

Raphael found that by using AI and machine learning, they could implant computer chips to target cancer cells in patients. These would recognize abnormal cells before they turned to cancers, and they programmed the computer chips to destroy them. The effect was to permanently eliminate the possibility of these abnormal cells invading tissue and becoming incurable. How Raphael's mind worked was nothing like anyone had ever seen before.

There was a ceremony at the University of Toronto to honor this outstanding achievement. His mother, Sophie, and his father, Gavin, were both there. There was another man called Wang, a Chinese national, who was the one who had contributed 50% of his genetics to him. Iona and Jeremy, whom he referred to as his grandparents, came as well. He had learned all about his creation as he grew up and knew that he was special. His life was just beginning, and everyone kept on telling him he would do great things. He knew he would not disappoint them.